The Christmas Tree Treasure Hunt

Joan Campbell,
Fay Lamb, Jennifer Fromke,
Deanna Klingel, Sheryl Holmes,
J.A. Marx, Ruth O'Neil, Debbie Roome,
and Marji Laine

W

The Christmas Tree Treasure Hunt
© 2019 Marji Laine Clubine
ISBN: 978-1-944120-84-9

This book is a work of fiction. Names, characters, places, and incidents are either products of the author's imagination or used fictitiously. Any similarity to actual people and/or events is purely coincidental.

Published by
Write Integrity Press, LLC
PO Box 702852
Dallas, TX 75370

Printed in the United States of America.

Table of Contents

Chapter One

Joan Campbell

"Sign on the dotted line," the FedEx man said in a bored voice as he handed me the box.

I scribbled my signature where his finger pointed and then turned my attention to the package I'd first thought had arrived for my roommate, Rebecca. It was one of those flat-rate boxes, and very light, almost empty, but not quite.

My name and address were written on its front in a flourished cursive that seemed strangely familiar. Where had I seen that handwriting before? Turning over the package to check the sender's name provided no clues; there was no return address.

I hurried inside and rustled through a drawer for a sharp knife. Still studying the white package in my hands, I flopped into the chair that caught the last of the day's sun and slid the knife into the tape covering the joints of the box. A surge of child-like excitement made me smile. Here I was, a twenty-one-year-old woman, as excited as a five-year-old opening a present from under the Christmas tree!

I'm not exactly sure what I was expecting, but this definitely was not it. Nine large manila envelopes were in the box, each labeled with a number from one to nine. What was this—a practical joke from a friend? Maybe it was one of those silly presents you had to unwrap layer after layer, only to discover nothing more than an Oreo cookie.

I tipped the envelopes onto the coffee table and was about to reach for the first one when I saw the corner of a cream sheet of paper peeping out between two of the envelopes. My hand trembled slightly as I reached for the letter and unfolded it. As my eyes took in the *Dear Gracie* at the top, shockwaves rippled through my body. A searing pain crept into my chest. Breathe. My mind had to tell me what my body seemed to have forgotten.

Gracie. Only one person called me that, and she had died five months ago.

My eyes travelled to the bottom of the page: *All my love, Grammie.*

I dropped the letter as if it were on fire.

Who? Who would do something this cruel? I could think of only one person who might want to hurt me this badly and that was Lauren. But I hadn't seen her for three years. She hadn't even had the decency to come to Grammie's funeral. Would Lauren go to such great lengths to hurt me? Again?

My shaky hands managed to pour a glass of water, and for the next ten minutes, I sat on the sofa, as far as possible from the letter and envelopes as I could be.

My mind was awash with memories of the past. The day Lauren disappeared without a trace, leaving only a small note telling Grammie not to worry. The day the rumours started at school– Lauren had left because she was pregnant, and the father of the child was Steve. Finding Steve, crying behind the rafters, and hearing it from his own lips: he didn't love me anymore. It was Lauren he loved; perhaps it always had been.

Three years later and I could still feel the twisted knot of their betrayal deep inside me. The last words I spoke to her were also crystal clear in my mind. A few days after high school graduation, I'd walked in to find her, heavy with child, weeping in Grammie's arms. The prodigal had returned. As our eyes met, she let out a startled cry and stretched out an arm toward me.

"Grace. Can you ever forgive me?"

I remember well the icy cold feeling that gripped me then and infused every word I spoke.

"No, Lauren. Never. In fact, I never want to see

you again."

I fled the house, and when I returned that night, she was gone. Over these last years, Grammie had tried, of course, to change my mind. Once she had even held out a picture of a smiling baby wearing a pink bonnet. "Look Gracie, it's . . ." But I had pushed away Grammie's hand. "Don't! Don't show me that."

Yes, Lauren had broken my world apart once before; I wouldn't put it past her to do it again.

When my heartbeat and breathing had returned to normal and my thoughts stopped their furious racing, I made a decision. My first instinct had been to burn the letter, the envelopes, even the box they arrived in. That way I wouldn't allow Lauren the pleasure of upsetting me any more than she had already. Yet, after I calmed down, I realized that I wanted to understand the game she was playing. I would read the letter, open the envelopes, and then decide how to proceed from there.

I picked up the letter and started to read.

Dear Gracie,

My darling, how I hope this letter hasn't upset you. By the time you get it, I will no longer be with you. The doctors are saying another month, maybe two at most. I knew I wouldn't make it until Christmas, so I wanted to give you one final gift. I hope it is the best one yet.

Do you remember when you and Lauren were little? One of your favorite games was our Christmas Tree Treasure Hunt. I remember how the two of you would come to visit us in December. You city girls loved the Colorado mountains, the trees, the forest trails. Gramps and I would set up a map, and you'd have to find each of the trees in which we'd hung one of the Christmas ornaments. Then, when you had all of them, we'd give you the last clue to the tree where the real prize was hidden. Do you remember, darling? And then on Christmas Day your parents would be there too. How precious those memories are to me.

Well Gracie, I want to send you on one last Christmas Tree Treasure Hunt. This one is a bit different. It's more spread out, in fact, and while you're looking for the Christmas ornaments, you'll also experience some people and places I wish I could have shown you while I was alive. Who knows? You might even uncover a secret or two.

In the box you just received are nine envelopes, and each one will guide you to a different place, with a different tree and a different ornament. Open the envelopes only when you're about to set off on the next part of the journey. It's kind of like your favorite show, the Amazing Race, right?

If my timing is right, you're in the middle of November now and you should be able to take a break from Southern Texas U without losing any credits. Also, if you're still working for Bertie, I'm pretty sure he'll give you six weeks off (although he'll moan like crazy). Just tell him I told you to do it—he's always had a soft spot for me.

There is so much to show you. I can't tell you how much fun I've had putting this together, and I want you to know that I'm with you every step of the way.

Are you ready for our last Christmas Tree Treasure Hunt, darling? Open your first clue—Envelope 1. And then let the adventure begin.

All my love,

Grammie

I must have sat with the letter in my hand for a very long time, because when I finally looked up, darkness had crept into the apartment. My skin had that stretched feeling you get when tears have dried, and there was a lump in my throat that I couldn't seem to swallow away.

The letter wasn't from Lauren. It was from Grammie, of that I was sure. Who else could come up with such a crazy, harebrained idea? Who else would even think of having me hurtle all over the place looking for trees and ornaments but Grammie, the most adventurous person I'd ever known?

I did remember the Christmas Tree Treasure Hunts. I also recalled just how much Lauren and I had looked forward to those special trips to Colorado. Yet, that had all changed when we were fourteen and our parents were killed on the drive up to the mountains.

I rose, pushing the intrusive thought aside, and feeling for the switch on the wall. As the light flickered on, I looked over at Grammie's box and the table strewn with envelopes.

Lately, I'd become rather adept at forgetting. I had thrown myself wholeheartedly into student life: studying, hanging out with friends, and partying, anything to forget the loss and pain of the past. But

Grammie's parcel changed everything.

I glanced at my watch. Seven o'clock. I was meant to be at Escalante's, for my roommate's birthday party. But with my puffy eyes and throbbing head, I was in no state to go.

I had a decision to make. Should I throw Grammie's box away, stuffing all the memories it had unlocked back deep inside me? Or should I open that first envelope and follow Grammie's clue to wherever it led? Could I risk letting in any more pain?

In the end, my love for Grammie helped me to decide. One sentence of her letter kept running through my mind: *I want you to know that I'm with you every step of the way.* In this final adventure Grammie had set up for me, I would have her by my side one last time.

So I tore open the first envelope.

Chapter Two

Ruth O'Neill

New York

I dumped the contents of the envelope onto the table, and they fell out with a clunk. I pushed aside the papers and smaller envelope to discover a credit card and key. Instinctively, I knew what it opened, but just in case I hadn't known, Grammie included a tag with "Home" written on it. The key was for the old farmhouse in Elbridge, New York, where we had lived before our parents moved us to Boston when I was eight. All the locks used skeleton keys unlike many of today's modern locks. I took a breath before unfolding the note then looked at Grammie's familiar handwriting.

Dear Gracie,

They say, "home is where the heart is." For this stop in your journey, I want you to go home. I hope you can find the child's heart you left there. I think you will be surprised at what you discover.

Love,

Grammie

P.S. I think there's enough on the credit card for your whole trip's expenses, as long as you don't start dining at five-star restaurants!

The three-acre plot we had lived on would always be home. That's where I remembered being the happiest.

Sighing, I looked at my watch. Too late to do much of anything but pack for now, I went to my bedroom to choose the warmest clothes I owned.

New York was cold in December. There would be much to arrange tomorrow. I'd have to talk to Bertie about taking a six-week break from work. I could just imagine his reaction to that. I'd also have to let the college admin department know I'd be back next quarter.

That night, I was too restless to sleep. I pulled out the scrapbook Grammie had made for my sixteenth birthday. I hadn't read it in a long time. As I opened the front cover, waves of emotion assaulted me. The thought came to me that Lauren had one just like it. Had she also tucked it away along with all the sadness of the past? I gazed at the pictures that told the story of my life from birth until then. Grammie said that we should add our own pages, but I didn't have the heart, not after Lauren left. Who knew so much would change in our lives that next year?

It took me two days to arrange everything. Bertie initially flew into a rage, but when I told him it was for Grammie, he softened and agreed to keep my job open until after the first of the year. With that—and all the college paperwork resolved—I could catch the morning flight out of Houston to Syracuse, New York. *This is a little crazy, you know that Grammie?* I must have said a few hundred times along the way.

By late afternoon, I had cruised through Elbridge and was finally steering the rental car into the driveway of our old home. *For Sale*—the sign stood boldly on the lawn. It seemed wrong that this sanctuary of my childhood memories could be traded by strangers. Pushing down the irrational resentment, I looked over to where the old barn used to stand. It had been a playground for Lauren and me when we were little girls, playing house, solving mysteries, and sharing daydreams of what we would become when we grew up.

I smiled. Lauren and I had planned to live near each other forever. We figured we started this life out in the same womb, so we were going to finish it as close as possible. I was going to use the barn foundation and build a house while Lauren would live in the main house. We would always be together, always there for each other.

Of course, all that changed the day Lauren and Steve betrayed me. Pushing down the anger threatening to surface, I walked toward the house, which appeared deserted—abandoned and lonely—much like I felt since Grammie died. I couldn't resist peeking into one of the ground-floor windows. Cobwebs fluttered where curtains used to hang, and the interior was dark and empty. I tried the front door, but it was locked. Grammie's skeleton key wouldn't work in the modern lock, so I didn't even try it.

I walked around the outside of the house, looking up to the second-story window of the room Lauren and I had shared. One of its walls had been covered with paintings of fairies and unicorns, horses, and princesses. "Paint is cheap," Dad used to say, and he and Mom had celebrated every picture painted by our hands as if Picasso himself had created them.

I spied the path that led through the woods. For old time's sake, I decided to take a little hike, but . . . each step further into the woods brought back more memories. I walked past the tree where we had pledged our commitment to be there for each other forever.

"Are you going to do it?" Lauren had asked.

"Why should we do that? I think it's stupid."

"To prove our promise to each other. We need to be blood sisters."

"We're already blood sisters. Everything about us is the same," I said.

In those days, my sister, my womb mate, had been my best friend, but who could have foreseen what was to come?

Not wanting to dwell on that memory, I quickly continued on the winding path through the woods. A breeze swirled around me, chilling me to the bone. I snuggled deep into my coat and remembered how Grammie had once walked down this path on a windy day, holding our two small hands in her own.

"Do you hear that?" she had asked.

"I hear the leaves in the trees," Lauren had answered.

"That's right. Do you know what they're saying?"

"Grammie," I said, "trees don't actually talk."

"Oh, but they do. They're singing and praising God, their Creator."

"Grammie, that's silly." Even Lauren had a hard time believing it.

"I'll show you the verse that proves it when we get back to the house."

At the end of the path was the hill where we used to take Grammie and Gramps on picnics when they came to visit. In the winter months, we would sled down that same hill and exhaust ourselves climbing back up, only to slide down again. We would do this over and over again.

I laughed out loud as I remembered the pricker bushes at the bottom of the hill. Somehow, Lauren always used to end up in their grasp. The briars would be stuck to her coat, her hat, and her hair, and Lauren would cry as Mom removed them. Lauren and I had raced down that rise during the other seasons of the year when no snow lay on the ground. I looked around, just to make sure no one was watching me, before throwing caution to the wind and running down—arms outstretched—like I used to do. I felt young and carefree once again. Back at the house, I read the other note Grammie had left for me in this package.

Dear Gracie,

I hope you have enjoyed your trek around the old home place. Sure brings back a lot of memories, doesn't it?

Now, do you remember the tree fort you

girls built in that huge maple in front of the house? I had a little help, so you should find a ladder to make your climb easier. I left a special gift for you there.

I love you,

Grammie

I looked to the front of the house. I had forgotten about the maple tree fort. In fact, there were two huge maples shading the house in the heat of summer. One of the trees stood closer to the road. That was the tree where Lauren and I had built our fort. The other tree was precariously close to the window of our bedroom. I took a deep breath and walked toward the tree fort. Then I climbed the ladder and sat down on the dusty platform. Another memory rushed back: Lauren screaming as her hair got caught in the tree branches. I tried to release her tresses but eventually had to fetch Mom, who had been forced to cut Lauren's hair free. I remember Grammie laughing on the phone and muttering something about Absalom in the Bible. It was about the only time in our lives that Lauren and I looked a little different.

A chilly breeze blew and fluttered the couple of leaves that were still hanging on for dear life. Something else moved in the breeze and caught my eye: a Christmas ornament. I reached out for it. Not just any old ornament, mind you. A "God's eye," just like the one Grammie had taught us to make one cold, blustery day when we couldn't go outside. After that, we had made one every year, taking small but sturdy branches from the tree, crossing them, and then wrapping various colors of yarn around them. Some years there were three colors, one representing each of us. Some years there were only two colors, representing my sister and me.

A single tear slid down my cheek.

Clutching the God's eye, I climbed down from the tree. I'd had enough of my visit to my childhood home. Even here, pain hovered around every corner. Driving back, the cheerful Christmas music grated on my nerves. I switched off the radio. Grammie always used to pray in the car, and for a fleeting moment, I considered doing the same. Then I remembered that God and I were not exactly on speaking terms. As the miles crept past, I tried—in vain—to capture all the memories this visit had unleashed and to push them back deep into the dark recesses of my heart. Another envelope awaited.

Chapter Three

J.A. Marx

Colorado

The view must be gorgeous, but I didn't dare take my eyes off the winding road. Everyone drove so fast up the narrow part of the canyon and even faster through the flat areas. I supposed if I lived in the Rocky Mountains, I would own a four-wheeler and drive that monster anywhere and in any way I pleased.

Finally, the last hill. I entered the valley, and the terrain spread wide before me. On my right, Lake Estes looked like the perfect ice bath. All those summers when we visited our grandparents, Daddy had taken us out there in sailboats.

A quick glance to the left and I saw Longs Peak glistening in the noon sun.

Wait! What was the mountain farther left? Excitement spiked my pulse.

Midway across the lake, I pulled to the side of the road and rolled down my window for an unobstructed view. A cold breeze seized my face and slithered around my neck. My breath came out in vapory wisps as I gazed at the mountain. Not just any mountain. The one in the picture Grammie had included in the envelope. I hadn't expected to find it this quickly.

The information for this leg of the treasure hunt was riding in the passenger seat under my purse. I took the envelope, slipped out the photograph, and held it up outside the window to confirm the identity. "That's it, Grammie. I found the mountain."

A whisper of fear shadowed my child-like

delight. Leaving my part-time job and taking off school to do a treasure hunt was insane. But I couldn't turn back now. I'd committed to this crazy adventure, and to leave it unfinished would mean dishonoring the woman who had loved and cared for me.

Grammie's letter instructed me to learn the name of the peak before driving to the address. Any local should know. After a quick visual search, I did a U-turn and headed back to the base of the hill leading to the canyon. I parked at the little motel located on the right.

A jingling bell announced my entrance into the lobby, and a thirty-something-year-old woman in a turtleneck sweater looked up from the reception counter.

"Good morning." She smiled, studying me intently. Her blue-tinted blond hair hung past her shoulders.

Bearing the awkwardness of her probing stare, I approached the woman with my photograph. "Hi.

I just have a quick question."

She leaned on the counter. "How much did you pay to get your hair that color? I love it. I've got to take a picture to show my stylist."

Warmth shimmied up my neck, defeating the chill caused by the weather. People often commented on how my tight auburn curls perfectly complemented my dark olive skin. And they all believed it to be fake.

I cleared my throat. "Thanks. It's natural. My mother was African-American. My father was white. Daddy gave me the bright red hair." Convinced that should satisfy the woman, I placed the photograph on the counter facing her. "Can you tell me the name of this mountain?"

"It's natural. Wow." It took her long enough to rip her gaze away from my features and look at the photo. "Oh, that's Twin Sisters." She pointed to her left. "It's right up the road."

Twin Sisters. A dull ache gripped my stomach. Out of politeness, I let the woman take a headshot of me with her iPhone. Pursing my lips to keep from screaming, my attempt at smiling for the camera failed.

I hurried to the car, buckled in, and let out a long screech. "This was cruel, Grammie. I know you didn't mean..." I gripped the wheel. "No, actually I don't know what you mean by this."

Lauren. Again. There could be no mistake at the implication in Twin Sisters.

Don't dwell on it. If I did, I'd talk myself out of this ridiculous treasure hunt.

Digging through the envelope and tearing the flap off in the process, I found the address.

45 Christmas Tree Lane. "You've got to be kidding." Was this place for real?

I punched the address into the GPS, which took me a few minutes to figure out. I'd never owned one of these gadgets since I could find my way around Houston blindfolded.

Fish Creek Road was the first segment and, strangely, just happened to be the road on which the motel was located. Had Grammie known I'd stop here? Not that Estes Park was a large place. But I'd heard mountain roads weren't necessarily marked as clearly as city streets and so opting for the GPS instead of a map seemed wise.

Traveling along the base of a mountain range took me farther away from the lake and the village. If it wasn't for the bitter thoughts hissing at me like vipers, I'd have probably considered this a pleasant drive.

A left turn placed me on Rockwood Lane. I slowed to a stop and peered out the windshield straight up at Twin Sisters towering above. My stomach growled, mostly from hunger but partially from irritation. Shaking my head and muttering mean nothings, I pressed the gas and proceeded at a worm's pace.

Was Lauren hiding up here? In a luxury cabin? In a teepee? In a cave with bears . . . waiting to be eaten?

My friend Kari, a psychology major, said

bitterness was going to kill me. Dr. Phil confirmed it on his television show. But I still couldn't stop nurturing my condemnation toward Lauren. She deserved the worst. Well, no, the worst was reserved for terrorists, but Lauren came in a close second.

Winding my way up the thickly wooded mountain, I found myself on Christmas Tree Lane. A road I'd never volunteer to tackle in the snow. As a two-story house came into view through the trees, I pulled over to check the envelope. Had Grammie forgotten any details? The note didn't say who lived here or what I was supposed to do except collect some ornament.

I'm with you every step of the way, her initial letter had said. If I listened hard enough, I could hear her voice whispering in my heart.

Kind of hoping not to be noticed, I rolled ahead and parked beside the wooden structure. The dirt-packed parking area seemed extra large, as if a family of twenty lived here. But I only saw one small SUV, durable enough to survive any snowy deposit.

Returning the picture and note to the ripped envelope, I stuffed it in my purse and opened the door. The rich scent of pine filled my nose. I could've stood there for a while enjoying the crisp air, except I feared getting in trouble for trespassing. Looking around for a privacy sign, I didn't see one.

I walked around to the front of the house, admiring the rustic décor on the porch. Two couch-length benches carved out of logs rested against the wall. Decorative, flat wooden panels underlined each plated window. A yard-high wooden figure of a bear standing on its hind legs waited at the front door.

I walked up the steps. "Okay, Grammie. Here we go." Pressing the doorbell set off chimes.

A few seconds later, an elderly woman in jeans and a long, button-up sweater swung open the door. Judging by the amount of wrinkles and liver spots,

I declared her a century old. But her perfect posture and bright eyes said half that. Thin silver tufts of hair licked at the air from under her granny skull cap, which looked homemade...and a lot like the crocheted caps Grammie used to wear in the winter.

The woman clasped her hands together at her chest, smiling brighter than the sun. "Grace. I was wondering when you'd arrive."

She knows me? Relief and apprehension toyed with my heart. Grammie wouldn't have sent me someplace unsafe. "I'm . . . it's . . . good to be in the mountains again." What a lame thing to say.

"Come in and warm up." The stranger stood back and beckoned with one hand.

Before stepping over the threshold, I noticed the colorful wooden sign above the door that said, HAVEN. A haven for what?

"Don't mind Rusty." She patted an elderly Black Lab wagging his tail. "He's a quiet sweetheart."

Quiet was right. I didn't notice the dog until

she mentioned him.

Rusty gave me his paw, and I scratched his ears. The aroma of a home-baked meal captured me the second the woman closed the door.

The spacious interior, lined with cozy rugs gave me a snuggly feeling. A feeling like I used to get as a child, cuddling with Daddy.

Mrs. Skull Cap directed me to a chair by the fireplace. "We have much to talk about, and I know you're on a tight schedule."

You do? I suddenly felt like Alice in Wonderland.

"But first, you have to try my new chili recipe. And afterward, some apple crisp." She walked to the kitchen attached to the large living room. "Your grandmother told me apples in any form are one of your favorite things."

I warmed my hands by the fire, reluctant to sit while an older lady served me. "So you know my grandmother."

"Oh, honey. Beatrice and I were best friends

back in elementary school." The woman maneuvered around her kitchen like nobody's business. "Bea was my maid of honor, and I would've been hers if my husband hadn't swept me off to Europe as an officer's wife. I'll be right back."

She disappeared into a back room, which gave me time to look around. Framed pictures on one wall drew me to peruse the faces. At least thirty, all with names on the bottom. Young people, mostly. Except for a handful of women who looked to be in their early thirties. I visually traced every face to the end of the collection—and did a double take.

Lauren's mug hung fourth from the end.

A sour taste seeped up my throat and lodged in my mouth. I wanted to spit on her face that had no right appearing so cheery. This explained why Mrs. Skull Cap recognized me without an introduction.

"You found your twin." The woman's sweet voice clashed with my mood. "We'd better get down to business. I'm sure you have a lot of questions."

Pressing my lips together to keep from saying something I'd regret, I joined her in front of the fireplace where she placed two bowls of chili and tumblers full of water. Sour cream and shredded cheese filled two smaller dishes.

I loaded both onto the chili and picked up my spoon.

"Heavenly Father," the woman said, head bowed.

Pausing out of respect, I puffed out a breath.

"Thank You for providing nourishment and for bringing Grace to the haven. In Jesus' holy name."

Skipping the amen, I stirred the cream and cheese into the beans.

"You haven't asked my name." The woman sprinkled a dainty amount of cheddar into her bowl. "Florence Crosby. Call me Flo."

You're such a twerp, Grace. Grammie had not taught me to behave like this. "Thanks for your hospitality, Flo. I'm sorry for my attitude. I'm still upset with my sister."

"Yes. I saw the pain in your eyes the second I opened the door. I'm glad God brought you here."

"I'm angry at Him, too." I shoved a spoonful of chili into my mouth but had to slow down to savor the zesty flavor.

"He's not angry with you, Grace. He misses how you used to sing love songs to Him every morning when you were first getting to know each other." Flo closed her eyes and bobbed her head as if hearing music. "Yes, He was just beginning to reveal Himself to you. His mysteries."

The lump in my throat grew bigger. How did Flo know about the songs? Not even Lauren or Grammie knew. I took a swig of water to wash it down. This lady was freaky.

"When Bea told me what happened to you girls in high school, I told her to send Lauren here."

I threw a sneer at the photos on the wall then returned to the chili. If I could demand the ornament and leave, I would.

"Your sister had nowhere to go. She was ready to take her own life."

That pricked my heart. I was angry at Lauren, but to think she'd take her own life would . . . would not bring justice. Halfway through the bowl of chili, I paused to take another drink.

"She was overwhelmed with humiliation and shame. The only thing that stopped her from suicide was not wanting to destroy the precious life she carried. She was going to put the child up for adoption."

Was going to? "So she kept it."

"Her."

"I guess she didn't throw all her responsibilities out the window. Like she did when Grammie died." Spite framed my words, but I didn't care. "I had to plan the entire funeral and take care of all the arrangements. Greet all the mourners by myself, and listen to their stories about Grammie. All that while Lauren ran off, probably with some new lover."

Not to mention she'd stolen my boyfriend.

"There was no lover, Grace. Lauren was raped. What you'd call a date rape, but rape just the same."

Flo's statement stabbed my heart like a dagger. The bowl dropped from my hands, thumped on the brown patterned rug, and tipped sideways. Chili spilled. Breathing suddenly became difficult.

I reached toward the mess I'd made. "I'm sorry."

Flo stopped me. "We'll clean it later."

If eyes could embrace, this woman had me in a bear hug. I couldn't pull away from her sea-blue gaze.

Rusty lumbered over and lapped at the lumpy slush.

"Lauren ran away out of fear."

I closed my eyes, straining to make sense of the news. Why hadn't Lauren said something? We were twins, for Pete's sake! We'd been tight. Even had our own stinkin' language . . . which had evaporated after Mom and Dad died.

This can't be. I rolled back into the chair, no longer hungry. "Lauren," I whispered, fighting tears.

Flo left again and returned with a square, wrapped box. She laid it in my lap.

Tracing the checked pattern with my finger, I felt undeserving of any gift.

"Open it, Grace."

I heaved a sigh and sat up. Removing the bow, I wedged it between my legs for safe keeping and peeled off the gold wrapping. The lid slipped off easily, and I peered inside at an ornament and another photograph. I studied the picture of Lauren holding a smiling baby.

"She delivered her here." Flo gestured toward the upstairs. "They spent a year with me."

I shifted my gaze toward the wall of photos, single mug shots of people in situations like Lauren had been. "That's what you do, isn't it, Flo? Take people in."

The old lady let out a sprightly laugh. "God

told me if I opened my doors, He'd bring 'em in. I wasn't able to have children of my own, and I wanted them so badly. When Hank died, bless his heart, I told God I didn't want to be alone."

This woman was growing on me.

"The local pastors bring people to the haven where I offer free room and board. In return, the girls help cook and clean, and the boys chop wood and do minor repairs." She smiled toward the wall of faces. "And my inheritance is growing."

If I were half as giving as this woman, I'd have a permanent halo. I lifted the ornament out of the box, and something stirred inside of me. Handcrafted pewter, perhaps? Circular, like a bracelet. Woven in the sides were three strands, braided together, wrapped in a full circle. The artistry was stunning. It hung from a silky periwinkle blue ribbon—the exact color I'd always called my favorite. Gram knew that too.

"Bea mailed it to me along with her request to give it to you."

I wasn't sure, but something told me this ornament would make sense as the treasure hunt progressed.

Chapter Four

Deanna Klingel

North Carolina

North Carolina? I'd never even been to North Carolina. Had she? What could possibly be here for me? I felt like I was spending my life packing and unpacking. I really wanted to just walk away, but I'd only just started. *Grammie, you knew I couldn't walk away from the Christmas tree treasure hunt, didn't you? You knew me too well.*

Welcome to North Carolina. The Great Smoky Mountains were nothing like the Rockies. The Smokies were greener, rounder, and softer looking, the vistas green and blue, more horizontal than vertical, more worn down, older, cozier. I pulled into the visitors' center at mile marker five, just where Gram's instructions said I should stop before heading into the nearby town of Rowland. As I drove toward the main building, I saw the strangest looking Christmas tree I'd ever seen. I parked and went to examine it up close. Beside me, a visitor studied the fragrant pine tree decorated with book covers as ornaments.

"Apparently all the writers from North Carolina decorate this tree every year," the stranger told me. "These are covers of their books. Interesting idea, isn't it?"

"Hmm. I guess," I answered indifferently.

He walked away, apparently having read all the book covers. *Maybe I'll find a good read.* I read the title on the cover dangling in front of me: *With or Without Her: A Memoir of Losing and Being a Twin*, by Dorothy Folz-Gray. My spit stuck in my throat, strangling me. Gram again? But she couldn't possibly have had anything to do with this. Could she?

I walked away from the tree to look at the maps on the wall, studying the area. The remoteness of the mountains and the chill in the air caused me to shudder. I helped myself to the free hot cider, another North Carolina gift to strangers. After gulping it down, I headed into town, eager to get this journey completed.

Finding a parking spot proved easier than it first appeared. For Rowland to be a small town, there sure was a lot of hustle and bustle. I turned off the ignition and stared up and down the main street of the quaint little village. Hearts-a-Bustin' vines tangled and twisted around the wobbly wooden fences enclosing small gardens in front of the shops. Bittersweet leaned against the shutters. Inside the fences, I saw the winter remnants of roses and herbs and the flopping heads of dried hydrangeas. I stepped outside the car and felt something bump against my leg. I quickly pulled back into the car then breathed a sigh of relief when I heard the meow of a domestic cat.

"Go away, kitty. Go home." I got out of the car, put the envelope in my purse, which I tossed over my shoulder, and tripped down the sidewalk. Up and down the street, the concrete bubbled and crumbled over the tree roots, which seemed to be winning the contest for property rights.

Something in each unique shop window caught my imagination. Under different circumstances, I'd probably find the place delightful. At last I spied the sign: "Bide Awhile Books."

When I opened the door, the tinkling of bells played an actual tune: *If I knew you were comin' I'd have baked a cake.* The old hardwood floor creaked with every step I took. The cat that had followed me down the street streaked in ahead of me and jumped up onto the counter. In a beam of sunlight, the dust motes danced, and the kitty washed his face. A curtain of bamboo beads rattled. A plump African American woman in a velour tracksuit stepped through the curtain, smiled widely, showing Betty White dimples. The tracksuit was Partridge Family vintage stock.

"Oh, you're Bea's Grace, aren't you? Just as beautiful as your Gram said you were. I'm Maddie. Let's go put on some tea." I followed her through the beads into a cozy reading room.

"I guess you're another friend of my grandmother?" I finally got around to the question after the friendly formalities and the tea was served. It was chamomile–my favorite. *Had she known?*

"Honey, your gram and I go way back. I mean *waay* back.

"How did the two of you meet?"

"Where do I begin?" Maddie took a sip of her tea as she considered her own question. "Our parents were friends before we were even born and—living on the same street—Bea and I grew up more like sisters than friends. You know your Gram was an only child, right?"

I nodded.

"Well, I was one of five children, and your Gram was drawn to our large, loud brood. So different from her own quiet house, I suppose. My mama used to say "You and Bea are double the trouble of all my other children combined." Oh, the mischief the two of us would concoct!" Maddie laughed. I wanted to ask her what kind of mischief, but she was already talking. "Bea would get that sparkle in her eye that meant she was thinking up a prank or two. She was incorrigible, she was."

There was a long pause as Maddie took another sip of tea and carefully replaced the cup on the saucer.

"She was a beauty, too. Like you. By the time she was sixteen, the boys were already flocking around her. I was a real plain-Jane and might have been jealous except that she just used to laugh at all the attention. It was her and me. Bea and Maddie. Best friends forever." Maddie shifted in her seat, the laughter on her face suddenly replaced by something more somber. "But then Eric changed everything."

"Eric?" I leaned forward. I'd never heard Grammie talking about an Eric before.

"Eric was my brother," Maddie continued. "Two years older than us girls. Suddenly, Bea wasn't coming to my house just to see me anymore. She started to change. Wearing a little bit of rouge on her cheeks, pretty dresses instead of torn jeans. She wanted to sit and talk with the older boys rather than play pranks on them." Maddie smiled, but there was sorrow in the smile. "I resented it. Jealousy, of course. I said things intended to hurt her, started to ignore her at school. It's hard to believe, but I cut my very best friend out of my life."

Until then I had been completely absorbed by Maddie's story, but at those last words, I stiffened as understanding dawned.

"Are you saying you and Grammie were like me and Lauren?"

"No, Grace. I just . . ."

"'Cause it's not, you know," I interrupted. "Lauren had a child with my boyfriend." Date rape–Flo's words rose up in my mind. Still, what was my sister doing on a date with *my* boyfriend?

"I know it's not the same, Grace." Maddie's voice took on a placatory tone.

"Your bout of teenage jealousy is a bit different from that kind of betrayal."

"Yes. Except we both lost our best friend."

"Anyway, so what happened?" I tried to cover up my embarrassing outburst. "Obviously, Grammie must have dumped him since my grandfather's name wasn't Eric." I laughed at my weak joke.

"They dated for four years before getting engaged." She swiped at a single tear streaking down her face. "And then Eric . . ."

"And then Eric went to Vietnam." She swallowed. "He didn't come back."

"Oh . . . I'm sorry . . . real sorry," I mumbled, suddenly ashamed at my hasty, harsh words.

"Bea was heartbroken. We all were. But instead of drawing together to comfort each other, we pulled even further apart."

A long silence stretched between us. Maddie stared blindly out of the window, lost in the past, and I fidgeted with the tassels on my handbag.

"So when did you and my grandmother meet up again?" I asked, just to break the jagged quietness.

"About ten years ago." The light was back in Maddie's eyes. "I heard a knock on the door, and there she was."

"Wow."

"She'd tracked me down across three states. And in some ways, it was as if we'd never been apart."

Maddie's chair leg scraped the floor. Her slippers made kissy sounds on the floor. She put her cup in the sink and left the room. Just like that, she left me sitting there.

"I'll be back," she called from another room.

"Make yourself comfortable." I replayed her words as the cat jumped into my lap and curled up. I stroked him, and he purred.

Outside the window, the sky was dimming. I imagined evening would come early up here. I could already see the first star surrounded by twilight. The kissy noises of Maddie's slippers snagged my attention.

"Well. Here I am. How about I fix us some soup for supper? It's good weather for soup, don't you think? You gather your overnight things while I lock up the shop. We'll go upstairs."

"Oh, Maddie, that's kind of you, but I don't mean to impose. I'd planned to get a room."

"Nonsense! You have a room right here. Now go fetch your things."

How much she sounded like my Gram. "…go fetch your things." Just like something Gram would say. So, of course, I did. She and the cat were waiting at the door when I returned. She locked up, and we went back through the beaded curtain and climbed a narrow stairway. At the top of the stairs, we walked into an open room softened by the natural light of early dusk.

"Like it?" she asked brightly. "Just had it renovated. Skylights. It's just right for me."

"It's wonderful," I said, and I meant it.

I looked around the small kitchen. Tilted on the top cupboard, photographs in dusty frames caught my attention: old hairdos, old style bikes, saddle shoes, heavy coats with big buttons. Old photos. A group picture. There was Maddie with Grammie. So young looking. And one of Grammie with a handsome man at her side. Eric.

Maddie didn't chat much during dinner, and I was grateful. The soup was delicious, and I told her so, but my eyes kept returning to the cupboard. So much loss: Eric, Mom, Dad, Grammie, Lauren, even Lauren's baby. I thought about the numbered letters yet unopened in my front seat. Was the future in any of them? Overwhelmed with sadness, I put down my spoon and wiped away the unwanted tears. Maddie pulled me to my feet, wrapped me in a hug, then led me down the hall.

"Here's your room," Maddie directed. "It's a pull-out bed. I've made it up for you. There's not much space in here with the bed out. All this stuff is my hobby. Don't mind it. Just push it aside and put your things wherever you like."

An array of glass balls, tiny paint brushes, and small bottles of paint were spread across the top of the chest. Partially finished projects seemed to abound. I picked up a ball and discovered it was a tree ornament, missing its gold cap. A rabbit and trees were painted on the ball. Actually, as I looked more closely, the rabbit and trees were painted inside the ball.

"Like that one?" Maddie asked. "It's not quite finished yet. I'm not sure I like it very much."

"It's lovely," I said. "How do you do that?"

"I put that tiny little brush into the opening and paint. Just like that!" She snapped her fingers, nothing to it. "The surprise, dear, is that it has to be painted backward. It's just reversed from normal painting, you see. Instead of painting a background, then the subjects, the subject has to be painted first with the background painted over it."

I followed that, but how complicated. Not a snap of the fingers at all. I fell asleep thinking about her craft, painting from the inside. When you start from the inside, the subjects are the most important feature. You have to complete them first. Everything else is secondary. *Start from inside*, I dreamed. *The subjects . . . complete the subjects . . .*

I woke to the sounds of a quiet house. I smelled coffee, so I got dressed and hauled my overnight bag into the kitchen, ready for departure. The table was set with bagels, pastries, and juice. Coffee cups sat on the counter next to the coffeemaker. On one of the plates was an envelope with Grammie's familiar scrawl. I set it aside, not ready to deal with more surprises, and made myself some coffee. Where could Maddie be?

I smeared some cream cheese on a toasted bagel half and opened the envelope, its instructions directing me back to the welcome center to find an ornament. I quickly scribbled a note to Maddie, promising to write her soon then cleaned up and hit the road once more. This time, curiosity spurred me on.

The welcome center was less busy this morning as I pulled back into the parking lot. No one stood around the tree as I hurried over to it. The twin book cover was not in the same place, so I had to look for it. I circled the tree and finally spotted it on the back side, a bit higher than it had been before. I looked around to see if anyone was watching, and seeing no one, I reached for the cover. Just behind it, a glass ornament hung with a tag that said, "For Gracie." I took it down and hurried to the car. A clear glass ball. Painted from the inside, a copy of a photo Grammie had taken one Christmas at her house. Lauren and me. Me and Lauren. Matching plaid ribbon headbands. Braces on our teeth. We were fifteen.

The round ornament twirled in my fingers. Lauren and Gracie. Gracie and Lauren. An everlasting circle. Side by side. Grace and Lauren. The subjects, the most important part of the circle, completed first, fill in the rest later.

I glanced out the car window as a doe and two fawns came out of the woods behind the center, walked the edge of the parking lot, then disappeared into more woods farther away. One fawn hesitated and looked at me then dashed after its twin. Snow began to fall, and I burst into tears.

Chapter Five

Marji Laine

Honduras

I leaned toward the window, peering past the plane's wing and onto the teal expanse below. The monochrome of the ocean resonated within my core. How long had I felt so empty? Maybe this had been a dumb idea. After all, I couldn't bring Grammie back.

Craving distraction and reassurance, I pulled out the note I'd found with my flight vouchers.

My dearest Gracie,

I'm so thankful you decided to go with me on this journey. Your next stop will be the Andorre Orphanage in Siguatepeque, Honduras. My good friend, Adriana Sebastian, will meet you. The prize you seek stands both distressed and nurtured between heaven and earth.

You loving and ever-present,

Grammie

Something about a suspension between heaven and earth sparked a memory, but for the life of me I couldn't make the full connection.

A phone number at the bottom of the page put me through to the orphanage, and a thickly accented male voice on the other end promised a car at the airport. At least I think he said something along those lines.

The memory knotted my stomach. What if he misunderstood and nobody showed?

I forced my head back against the rest and

closed my eyes, trying to slow my nervous heart rate and calm my breathing. Surely, this large city had a taxi service to get me to the orphanage. And I could sleep almost anywhere for just one night. No problem. Nothing would keep me from finding my hidden treasure.

For an instant, I imagined Lauren sitting next to me and the giddiness we felt hunting as kids. The moment didn't last. Instead it stirred up painful visions of her betrayal.

Maybe I should have thought twice about going on Grammie's voyage.

After an introduction to the sweltering heat on a walk from the plane to customs, I collected my rolling suitcase out of a stack against the wall and headed for the exit. A tall, heavyset woman with lily-white skin and curly gray hair came directly toward me. "You must be Gracie. I'm Adriana."

She gave me a tight hug and led me to a rundown fifteen-passenger van with Spanish words across the side. "You're exactly like the picture your grandmother sent. I would have known you anywhere."

Good thing because I would never have picked out Adriana as a missionary to a Central American country.

Her speech held only a hint of accent, and she didn't seem to need any encouragement to keep up the conversation. "I told the children you were coming, and they are so thrilled. Anything and anyone new throws them into uproar, and this treasure hunt . . . well, they've gone right over the edge of excitement." She chuckled and shifted lanes. At least they looked like lanes, though few cars actually used them.

"The kids don't get to leave the village most of the time, far too dangerous, you know. The murder capital of the world they call this country now. Not that the drug cartels would be interested in a busload of kids, but I don't take the risk."

The thought of being in the murder capital of the world caught my attention with a nausea that crept into my stomach. Good thing I didn't have to test the *I can sleep anywhere* claim.

Adriana must have noticed my concern. "No worries. Everything we need, we can make ourselves or purchase in Agurramundo, the little village where we're headed."

"I thought your orphanage was in Sique . . . Sepet . . ."

"*Cigar-tea-pick-eh*. On the outskirts, and we avoid the city. Too easy to get lost."

I felt lost already. A scooter veered in front of us, coming inches from being squished. I braced my hand on the van roof, and Adriana honked the horn, but continued her chatter, almost oblivious to the unruly traffic and life-threatening near misses.

Leaving San Paulo Sula, she changed her topic to the surrounding land and distant mountains. Scars from the recent earthquake marked the landscape. Huge chunks were missing from the road and sections of small buildings were cracked or broken away. In one case, an entire bridge lay crumpled on the riverbed.

My thoughts spiraled inward. Broken. Missing pieces. I could empathize with this land.

Adriana caught me looking at the bridge. "Several cars fell when the bridge went down. I have one little boy who lost his entire family there. I still don't know how he survived. Most of them didn't."

"That's terrible." And it hit too close to my own tragedy.

"Not so terrible. He found Andorre."

I glanced back at the wreckage. Thankfully, I'd had family to fall back on. "How did you know Grammie?"

"Oh, now, that is a story, and an old one. Your grandparents had only been married a year when they came down here with a group from their church. They worked for over a week to put up the first building. It's one of our classrooms now, but then it served as an office, meeting room, even a bedroom during the rainy season before we built the dormitories."

"They helped you build it?" Had they ever told me about this place?

"From the very foundation. And they visited several times to help teach."

I could imagine Grammie with the children much easier than I could envision her holding tools.

We turned onto a dirt road skirting the edge of a village and came upon a cluster of bleached white adobe buildings huddled against the rock edge of a mountain. "This is it." My chauffeur pulled in front of the largest building as a dozen or more children of various sizes came running.

Opening her door, Adriana spoke to them in a smooth staccato. A boy pushed his way through the others then tugged at my door. I climbed out, instantly surrounded by kids, their hands stroking my scrunched auburn hair.

Though not tender-headed, all the fingers clawing through my tangles freaked me out a bit. "What are they doing?"

"I don't think they've ever seen hair such as yours." Adriana pulled out my suitcase and rolled it toward the house next to the largest building. "You'll be staying with me. I'll be back in a few minutes to rescue you."

"Rescue me?"

Her word-choice made sense after a moment. The children literally pulled me along, speaking as though I understood. The anxiety I'd felt during the journey lifted with the bright faces and uninhibited joy. A little boy with one of his front teeth missing spread out a wide smile and dropped a soccer ball in front of me.

Surely, they didn't mean for me to play? I glanced down at the low-heeled shoes I'd chosen for traveling. Oh well, the band across the middle would keep them on my feet. I settled my mouth in a determined smile and shoved the cuffs of my blouse over my elbows.

The kids cheered as I dug the toe of my pump into the ball and sent it flying across their makeshift field. The fact that I had no idea who played on which team didn't matter.

My kick sent several of the fastest runners after the ball, some trying to advance but more working on the return. A large group of girls jogged with me, watching and grinning. The attention delighted me, making me forget for a moment my missing grammie, the loss of my parents, even my bitterness toward Lauren.

The play came back after a few moments. I hoped to give the ball another good poke, but a speedy fellow got to it first. I kicked air, lost my balance, and toppled to my behind. The girls around me fell as well, erupting in fits of giggles. I couldn't remember the last time I laughed so hard about nothing.

Adriana and a shorter man came running across the field. The man reached me first.

"*Señorita*, are you all right?"

"I'm fine, just playing Charlie Brown." I giggled again and the kids joined me, though I knew none of them understood the joke.

Adriana introduced the man as Maxwell, the teacher at Andorre. He helped me up, but he looked nothing like a teacher, sporting long, shaggy hair, a gray shirt, and khaki shorts that had seen better decades. Was he even out of his teens?

"If you would accompany us." He spoke with the accent that I recognized from the phone conversation. "The students have something special that they would like to share with you."

"Yes, of course." I fell into step with Adriana and followed her inside the smallest building. "This is the section your grandparents built. Their team laid the foundation and braces to frame the walls."

Though wishing I'd been able to visit here with Grammie, I felt grateful that I could see the difference that her and Gramp's actions had made in the lives of these children. Desire to somehow make an impact ignited in my chest. Maybe not here, but somewhere.

The teacher arranged the children into rows. A tall girl, probably one of the oldest, explained in hesitating English, "By Robert Frost."

Together they recited a poem I'd known all my life. Despite the mispronunciations, Grammie's own voice rang through the words, as they had at her kitchen table years ago.

Two road diverged in a wood, and I . . . I took the one less traveled by and that has made all the difference. When they finished, I clapped long and hard, warmth growing in my heart over the preparation these precious children had put into giving me such a special gift.

A little girl stepped out of the front row, her chin tilted downward, making her huge dark eyes look even larger. I grinned at her, and with a slight smile, she held out a piece of folded card stock.

The words *Your Quest* printed on the outside in Grammie's unmistakable script stirred excitement. I opened the card expecting instructions. Instead I found a photo of Grammie and Gramps, much younger, standing next to a beautiful waterfall.

I turned the photo around and showed the kids. "Do you know where this place is?"

They started giggling, and several ran from the room. Did they even understand me, or did they want another soccer game?

One glance at Adriana's stoic face proved she didn't plan on explaining.

Maxwell finally broke the silence, nodding. "I do, though I'm not sure how much I should help." He left with another group of students in his shadow. I had no choice but to follow him.

We crossed the playing field, and he paused at a treed area on the downslope. I stepped closer and viewed a well-worn trail leading down the mountainside.

"Here you are, Dorothy." Maxwell laughed. "May you find your Emerald City."

"Very funny." I took the lead and tried not to stumble in my heels. "I guess you all walk this way often?"

"Often." The boy-man smiled again, offering nothing else.

"How long have you been at Andorre?" Might as well make conversation along the way. Maybe I could learn a little more about the place I sought.

The smile dropped off his face. "I have been here for a very long time."

So he'd been an orphan here. I didn't miss his guarded expression and chose a different, less upsetting topic. "How long have you been a teacher?"

"I took classes over the Internet last year, but I have been teaching here since *Señor* Sebastian died two years ago. *Señora* couldn't do the teaching and everything else required, so I stayed behind to help her."

"Stayed behind?" I wondered how he'd lost his family but didn't ask.

"Usually when the students come of age, they get jobs in the village. There are many there grateful to Señora and willing to find work for us."

Adriana obviously did a fine job with the children.

Passing a small glade with high grasses on both sides of the trail, we reentered the forest, and a thin path veered off to the left. The loud echo of crashing water drew me along the main walkway. After a short downhill trek, I came out of the forest to a magnificent view. The mountain stretched almost straight upward from where I stood. A cascade of fierce water fell from the sheer cliff above, landing in the blue-green pool just below me.

Pulling out the picture, I tried to match the place where my grandparents stood. Far closer than my view at the bottom, they seemed to be near the middle or the top. I gazed upward and recognized the spot right away. About halfway up the cliff, a thick ledge held a large tree. Rushes of the waterfall sprayed the tree and occasionally cut through its branches. I checked the photo again and could see just where my grandparents had stood.

Grammie's words from the note came back for further confirmation. *Both nurtured and distressed.* The tree stood, pounded by the very thing that kept it alive and made it strong. I'd found my treasure.

Pointing to the tree, I turned to Maxwell. "How do I get up there?"

He shrugged. "You took the wrong road."

Of course! The poem had a purpose, too. I'd barely glanced at the little path when I came into the woods, but I dashed back up the trail puffing hard. Alone this time, I took the narrow fork that led steeply upward.

I broke through the forest cover, sharing the cliff with the wounded tree. A light mist wet my cheeks and hair as I glanced over the side. Fear gnawed at my belly from the unprotected height, but a sparkle drew my attention to a low-hanging limb on the tree.

Ignoring the spray and the distant land below, I inched closer and collected the ornament, a hand-carved cross, rough-cut, with a gold crown about the size of a ring looped around the middle. Grammie's message came through. The tree stood lifted between heaven and earth just like the cross.

I held the treasure up. "I found it."

The group below cheered.

Moments later, I joined Adriana on the return trek to the orphanage. "It's hard to believe the children here have had such trouble. They seem so happy."

"They are happy. The depth of their pain makes them enjoy the good times. It's like that tree."

"Made strong and nourished by the beating of the water." I pushed out of the brush onto the playing field. Wide lines of sunlight crossed the expanse, announcing the coming sunset.

"Your grandmother told me you were smart. She also told me that your history holds experience much like my children."

I nodded in silence. I'd always thought I'd lost everything the day my parents died. But not like these kids. I'd always had Grammie and Gramps. And Lauren. Had my tragedy made me strong, too?

That topic needed more thought.

Chapter Six

Sheryl Holmes

Massachusetts

Boston, Massachusetts, evoked a myriad of memories for me. It seemed natural for Grammie to send me here. Having lived here from the age of eight, I looked forward to the familiarity of the city.

The gusty wind took me by surprise. I had forgotten how voracious the wind could be in the city as it rushed between the tall buildings, turning unbuttoned coat flaps and anything not tied down inside out in its fury. I made my way to the curb and hailed a taxi while mustering up every ounce of energy to keep my balance as the winter weather encircled me.

"Where to, ma'am?" the aging taxi driver inquired.

I searched my memory for a place to grab a quick bite to eat. "Take me to the corner of West Street closest to the Boston Common, please."

Surely, I could find a cheap place to eat on West Street. It was hard to know exactly what restaurants would have endured the recession over these last few years.

As we approached the Boston Common, camera shots flashed through my memory with vivid color as I recalled walking through the park in different seasons. Delicious green grass in the midst of the stark glass and concrete of the city rambled and beckoned to all who desired to frolic in the warmer months. The sweet memories of romping with Lauren flooded my mind, but I shook them away. *Stop! Grace, just stop it!*

Thankfully, the cabby's voice broke through my inner turmoil. "Here we are, West Street by way of Boston Common. That'll be eight fifty, ma'am."

I stepped out into the winter whip of weather in search of an affordable eatery. I plunged my hands into my pockets to keep the wind from turning my coat inside out, my hand securing the envelope inside. The signage for Max & Dylan's Kitchen caught my eye, and I seated myself at a table by the window as I perused the menu.

"What'll it be, sweet lady?"

Was this Max or was this Dylan? Good looking either way. "Just a flatbread sandwich with extra sprouts and avocado, please. Oh, and a hot cup of chamomile tea, too! Thanks."

The smell of garlic and warm yeasty bread filled the air. The place was small and trendy and the warmth from the ovens caressed my face. As I stared out the window, I was invited into a moment of remembering. *Oh, Grammie. Why did you have to die on me?*

Not too far away, Boston's hospital district stood tall and proud. It was almost a city unto itself.

She had the best doctors, but there was not much left to do but keep her comfortable as the cancer continued to ravage her body. The day she left me was grafted into my memory as a haunt.

Grammie, so frail and weak. Her soft skin hung like drapes on her bones. The cancer had metastasized and flowed like a savage victor through her body. Even though her eyes were sunk into the bone structure of her face, they danced and sparkled with expectation. I sat close on the edge of her bed as Grammie held my hand and reminded me of her final destination. "The Good Lord is preparing me a place Grace, and I don't want you to worry." Moments later, her eyes closed, and she rested in waiting. I watched over her as if in my presence I could slow down the inevitable. Her breath was so shallow as I listened and waited to see the blankets rise and fall like the gentle ripples on a still lake. Quiet. Oh, so quiet. My heart aching, I stood to stretch and then repositioned myself on the chair next to her bed. I drew my legs up and wrapped my arms about me in an attempt to feel a hug. Chin on my knees, I drifted off to sleep.

With a start, I woke to the raspy sound of Grammie asking for water. "I am so thirsty, Grace." As I handed her the tepid water, she thanked me for staying close by. "Grace, promise me you will reach deep into your heart and reconcile with your sister one day. If you don't, your anger will eat at you more aggressively than my cancer. Find the love again, Grace. Find the love."

Grammie, how could you ask it? I fought back the tears and tried desperately to swallow the lump in my throat to no avail. A single drop trickled down my cheek, and I swiped it away as if it were poison on my skin.

Grammie's breath suspended as if caught up in the air itself. A rise, but no fall. I knew right then that she was gone. Wishing to speak to her just one more time, I leaned down and pressed my cheek against hers and whispered into the stillness of the room, "I love you, Grammie!"

Totally unaware that I had drifted so far from reality, I startled as Max, or Dylan, placed my plate of food and tea upon the table in front of me with a cheery, "Enjoy!" I wriggled out of my coat and emptied my pockets onto the table: cell phone, gloves, and the envelope.

This was the fifth envelope. What a pleasant surprise it was to find the ticket when I opened the envelope two days ago. One choice seat. Front row balcony, center seat. My favorite view within the Boston Opera House. "Thank you, Grammie." This had been one of our special traditions: Grammie accompanying us to The Boston Ballet's Nutcracker at the opera house. Oh, too many years had passed since I was allotted this luxury.

I savored the last delectable bite of my sandwich and tea. Haphazardly checking my phone, I realized I had lingered too long. Now I risked being late! Slapping a twenty on the table, I more than covered the cost of my food and left a ridiculously sizeable tip for Max, or Dylan, to save myself time.

I ran toward the theatre district. When I rounded the corner onto Washington Street, the dropping temperatures smarted my eyes and made them tear. Through blurry vision, I saw the familiar old grandeur of the opera house just a hundred feet farther ahead. Majestic it stood; the buildings on either side paled in comparison. As a child, I felt like a princess entering a palace with all its ornate gold filigree designs.

As I handed my ticket to the well-dressed usher, I heard the familiar overture of Tchaikovsky's Nutcracker music. Rum, pum de— pum de-ata . . . I could hum that music any day! Though the curtains were still drawn, I envisioned the set of the living room and the gaily Victorian dressed dancers ready to enter the party on stage. Apologizing all the way past five or six already seated patrons, I found my seat and settled back, my face aching from smiling so big. The rush of the day ended and I revelled in the beauty of the dancers performing my most treasured ballet.

Elegantly dressed adult dancers enacted the party scene. Herr Drosselmeyer, the mystical uncle, gifts dear sweet Clara with a Nutcracker doll and she's overjoyed, as I would have been too. In a jealous fit, her brother Fritz stole the doll and smashed its cracker lever. Devastated and inconsolable, Clara wept in despair even as Herr Drosselmeyer tried to fix poor Nutcracker. *Oh how I love this story! This envelope destination is a natural fit, Grammie."*

Despite my old age of twenty-one, I found myself giddy as an eight-year-old, completely enamored with this tradition. I was once again mesmerized as the chiming of the grandfather clock began the count to twelve. Time stood still and my anticipation rose. The stage lights dimmed, and the magic began as the wee six-foot decorative Christmas tree grew and grew and grew. My back straightened as the tree grew taller and taller. Practically forty feet tall, the lights shimmered and this glorious tree captured the attention of the entire opera house! Pure enchantment filled the air. Clara's dream began.

Grammie's words came to me as plain as day. "Now, girls," she would whisper every year, "as awesome as this tree is, I want you to know that God is even awesome-er! He is sooooo big and yet He cares for each of you and even for your old grammie, too. When you ask for His love, He will fill you right up with it, and you will shimmer and light up just like this tree!"

Lauren and I had never given her our full attention since our eyes had been glued to the enormous tree. Yet I remembered the lesson Grammie taught us so poignantly, year after year. Tradition is good. No, it is excellent.

The soldier and mouse battle scene blurred by, The house lights came up as Act One ended and my bladder was just about to burst. Good tea. Yep– really good tea! I excused myself down the aisle of seats and found my way to the ladies' room.

Just as expected, there was a line. Always a line. The awkward type where everyone stands trying not to make too much eye contact with anyone. Polite smiles and minor comments abound, "Are you in line?" *Do people really have to ask?*

Only three people were ahead of me now, and a little hand poked out from underneath one of the stall doors.

"Mommy, I want to go out," a child voice pleaded. "Out there, Mommy."

"No, just wait a minute, Sweetie."

I chuckled with the rest of the ladies waiting in line. Cuteness is an easy icebreaker.

"But Mommy . . ." the child persisted. Silence. For just a minute. Then, as quick as could be, that little girl-child attached to the child-voice pleas scooted out from under the stall door with ease and agility.

"Clara Grace!"

The name filled the room with a tension only kids truly know. The hair on my neck stood straight up. When a mom used the first name accompanied by the middle name . . . *Oh dear little girl, this can't be good for you.*

An empty stall opened up, and I moved to it. As I passed by the little girl, I noticed a well-loved stuffed animal held fast in her arms.

The little girl and her mom were gone by the time I exited the restroom. The lights flickered that intermission was almost over, and I rushed to reclaim my seat.

Glad for my agility, I again made my way past the several sets of knees to reach my seat. The glitter of a gold bow caught my eye. *How odd.* I raised eyebrows toward my seat neighbors, silently asking if this box belonged to either of them. Each shook their heads, denying any claim to the small package. I picked it up then settled in my seat, totally piqued with curiosity. Ever so gingerly, I untied the sparkling gold bow, and it fell gracefully into my lap. Lifting the cover, I knew in an instant that this was another ornament carefully selected for me by Grammie; Simple, yet exquisite, the handblown glass formed a tiny replica of the massive Christmas tree on stage. I could hear Grammie's voice in my head again, "As awesome as this tree is . . . God's is even awesome-er . . ." As the house lights dimmed and the music began, I pondered only one thing: *who put this box on my seat anyway?*

My eyes returned to the stage just as Clara was ushered into the Land of Sweets, and I mused about the little escape artist, Clara. I remembered how much Lauren and I had loved the character of Clara in this ballet. We had gone home after each performance and pranced around in our nighties, envisioning ourselves as graceful ballerinas dancing with our Nutcracker. We had even made a pact that the first baby girl born from one of us, hers or mine, would be named Clara. Pinky sworn and sealed with spit! This was for real.

The rest of the ballet enthralled me, but before I knew it, I was again out in the cold hailing a taxi.

I never liked this part of city life. Walk and freeze or stand halfway in the middle of the street, risking life and limb, waving like a nut to ride in an ugly yellow car. Winter in Boston was, and always will be, unforgiving. Taxi secured, I whipped the side door open. "Copley Square Hotel, please."

Contentment filled me as the heat blasted in the car, and I recalled my evening. "Thank you, Grammie, for this wonderful night." Visions of prancing around in my nightie re-entered my mind. I could hear my mother and Grammie laughing with joy as they watched Lauren and me flit gracefully around our room. "Ballerinas? You think so?" they teased. "You're just two little monkeys dancing on the bed!" Monkeys . . . oh yeah, the monkeys Grammie made us for Christmas became our shining Nutcrackers as we danced! Sock monkeys. Memories rushed forward from the recesses of my mind.

The warmth and rocking motion of the cab lulled me into a light sleep. It had been a long day.

I bolted upright, all sleepiness vanished. "Monkeys!" I spoke aloud and caught sight of the taxi driver's surprised glance in the rear-view mirror. A nut. *Yup, he's thinking I'm a nut!* No matter. Thoughts took command. The old-fashioned sock monkey, just like the ones Lauren and I used as stand-in Nutcrackers, had hung limply in the arms of that little escape artist named Clara. I smiled, thinking about her again–the rambunctious child who entertained me in the restroom tonight.

But then . . . Clara Grace!

Clara Grace? Could it be . . .? No. Just a strange coincidence! But hadn't Grammie always said "There's no such thing as a coincidence"?

Time stood still once again, and breathing seemed impossible. Certifiable. I am sure the poor taxi driver thought I'd lost it.

Like an angel coming to minister, the words of Grammie echoed in my head, "Find the love again, Grace. Find the love."

Chapter Seven

Fay Lamb

Florida

The St. Augustine Lighthouse. Such a difference from all the mountains I'd seen lately. *Wonder why Grammie sent me here?* A briny breeze sent my skirt billowing.

Towering oaks surrounded the gift shop. I peered through crooked limbs to view the lighthouse, its brilliant red lens house sitting atop a barber pole striped tower.

I shut the door of my rental car before crossing the parking lot to the gift shop where the sunset tour would begin in less than five minutes. A gaunt man wearing suspenders, a twinkle in his aged blue-green eyes, opened the door for me. "Welcome."

"Thank you." I eased past him and stopped in front of a potted evergreen decorated for Christmas. A sign stated the nautical-themed ornaments had been donated by Friends of the Lighthouse. I touched one of the antique hand-painted lighthouses hanging on the tree. I'd seen an ornament like these before. Had Grammie sent me here for one?

I seemed to be the only visitor. "Where is everyone? Isn't the tour about to start?"

His brows drew together. He nodded. "Matt will be your tour guide. He's a bit cheeky, but he knows the history of the old place better'n I do. Should be back in a second. He's running an errand."

Beyond the french doors on the other side of the building, a white-haired woman approached. She shaded her eyes with a trembling hand against the glass and peered inside.

"That's Mrs. S." The man straightened a shelf of books on local history.

The woman searched the store until her gaze met mine. Then she smiled, waved, and walked away.

"Sorry I'm late." A young man rushed into the shop. He skirted the display racks of souvenirs specially designed for lighthouse tourism. At the register, he stopped, took a deep breath, and gave me a lopsided smile. "Hello, Grace. I'm Matt, your guide."

I blinked. "You know my name?"

He stared at me for a long moment, his gaze hinting of a secret known only to him. Then he looked down at the registry and ran his index finger along the only name. "Got it right here."

"You stayed open for me?"

Matt furrowed his brows, and for a moment, with his similar puzzled look, I thought he and the older man could be related. "No, we kept it open for a group." He half-chuckled. "You're the best-looking group I've led in a while."

Cheeky. The older man had it correct. I looked to find him, but he had left. Snarky. That's what my generation would call Matt.

"Let's get started." Matt pretended to put something over his short-cropped blond hair. "Officially changing hats from errand boy-slash-cashier to tour guide."

I smiled. How could I not. Matt was fun, and this was going to be an enjoyable treasure hunt. "Errant boy, maybe."

Matt pointed to me as he opened the door. "I like you."

As I exited the gift shop, I touched a poster for the lighthouse's Dark of the Moon tour. "Do you lead this one as well?"

He nodded. "It's our most popular event."

"So tell me, Matt, do you believe in ghosts?"

Matt's lopsided grin widened. "Of Christmases past, maybe. Though, there's a crazy woman around here who claims the grounds are haunted by a ghostly pelican."

I gave him my best smirk, unable to tell if he was joking. "A ghostly pelican? That's unique."

Matt led me down a sidewalk path hedged on each side by azaleas and oaks.

When I stepped outside, the fiery sun sat low on the horizon. I looked up at the spire of the lighthouse and caught my breath. Rays of brilliant light splayed from the lens house.

Matt stopped beside me. "Beautiful, isn't it? Been here before?"

"No. Grammie told me she and Gramps honeymooned here."

Matt led me to the base of the tower. He pulled a large ring of keys from his pocket and unlocked the door. "Ready for a workout? Two hundred nineteen steps to the top and what looks to be one of the prettiest sunsets I've seen."

Another Christmas tree decorated in similar fashion as the one in the gift shop stood against the wall in the rotunda. I fingered the green branches. Would I find Grammie's treasure on this tree? Or the one in the shop?

Matt drew my attention to a cistern in the middle of the room. With little interest, I leaned over the wrought-iron railing surrounding it. I didn't expect the well to hold anything Grammie sent me to find. I wanted to get to the top.

Halfway up the spiraling steps, I wondered if Grammie sent me here to meet the Lord—personally. My legs wobbled like jelly outside the jar. I failed miserably in my attempt to breathe evenly. By the third landing, I was ready to stop.

As if he knew I needed the break, Matt halted by an opened window. A stiff sea breeze gusted against my face, providing a coolness not found on the grounds. I leaned through the narrow slit, taking a deep breath. The air was heavy with brine.

Down below, the old man and the white-haired woman stood on an open area of the path. The lady pointed up. They both waved.

I reached through the opening and sent them a wordless hello with a return wave.

Matt leaned out beside me, his arm nudging mine. He looked around then ducked back inside with a shake of his head. "Okay, lazy bones, are you ready to make it to the top?"

I nodded. I'd kept in good condition—but not in stair-climbing shape. I grasped the railing and lagged behind Matt as he regaled me with the history of the first lighthouse built by the Spaniards, and this, its sturdy replacement. He beat me to the top and waited before pushing open the door.

I stepped out onto the iron platform below the beacon and gawked at the panorama unfolding before me.

A wind gust tugged the door from Matt's hand, pushing me sideways. "Careful there, klutz." Matt reached out and grasped my arm, his touch gentle. And that twinkle in his eye captivated me. After all, old men who knew the mysteries of life—those were the eyes that twinkled—not someone my age.

"Hey, buster. Watch who you're calling names."

Matt's laughter languished on the breeze. "Be careful. Hang on to the railing, and enjoy the sunset. I'll share more history afterward."

I strolled the platform, enjoying the view of Anastasia Island to the south, the Matanzas River and old St. Augustine to the west, the historic homes dotting the landscape to the north of the lighthouse, and the white-capped Atlantic Ocean to the east. Completing the circle, I stood beside Matt. I still labored to breathe following our climb as the fiery ball slipped below the horizon, leaving behind splashes of amber and pink against the twilight blue sky. The rotating beam of light above us cut into the deepening darkness.

"The lens is a Fresnel . . ."

"It's okay." My words passed quivering lips. "This is enough." I lifted my hand out to the beauty around me. "Grammie used to call us"—I cleared my throat of emotion—"my twin sister, Lauren and

me, outside just to say good-bye to the daylight."
The wind whipped my skirt, and I clasped the fabric
in my hands. Sometimes I missed Lauren as much
as I missed my grandmother. "So, tell me, Matt.
What makes someone as young as us hang out at a
lighthouse?"

Matt leaned his hip against the railing and
turned to face me. "Finding our way."

I blinked at his too-perfect description of my
journey.

"I took a detour and found trouble," he
continued. When I stepped back on the lighted path
the Lord had for me, I was determined to get back
to my roots. So, I found my grandfather. He was
one of the last lighthouse keepers who lived on the
grounds."

I was glad for Matt, glad he had found his way
back to his grandfather and to the Lord. But I had
lost that path a long time ago. And there was no
light in sight to guide me back to it.

Then I thought of my sister. What if Lauren

was having trouble finding her way as well? Grammie and I were all the family she'd had, except for the baby. I'd been angry with Lauren for her failure to return home for Grammie's funeral, but maybe I'd stood in Lauren's way. She couldn't find her way home because of my anger. Had I darkened the path for her?

Matt raised his arm, refocusing my attention, and traced the long beam with his finger. "For hundreds of years, this light or one similar to it has been a beacon in the darkness to sailors and landlubbers alike."

Unbidden, a long-forgotten memory verse stole into my mind. "I am the Light of the world. Whoever follows Me will never walk in darkness, but will have the Light of Life."

I shook my head to rid my mind of the intrusive words. Where on earth had *that* come from? And what did it mean? That all I had to do was follow Jesus and my life would be flooded with light again? Yeah right. If only life was that simple.

Matt touched my arm. "Ready?"

A moment crept by before I forced myself from my reverie. When I looked at Matt, warmth glowed in the depths of his blue-green eyes. "We have an exhibit in the keeper's house I think you'll find interesting."

I clopped down the iron steps of the well-lit tower right on his heels.

Matt escorted me across the courtyard and into the ground floor of the building there. "Not the same place Pops lived. That burned down in the 70s, but let me show you this." He led me to a Plexiglas and wood case. I ran my hand along the clear top as I perused the items from left to right. At the end, I stopped, looked closer, and turned to Matt.

His raised eyebrows told me he'd been waiting for me to make the discovery.

"May I hold it?" I asked, breathless. Grammie was so full of surprises, and this had to be a clue to the ornament I'd been sent to find.

"Since my family loaned it to the museum, I don't see why not." He pulled out his keys and slipped one into the lock on the side. After sliding the lid to the left, he pulled out my treasure.

My hands shook as I held the paper filled with Grammie's familiar scrawl.

Dearest Lester and Henny:

Your beautiful gift arrived today. It was a special reminder to us of our honeymoon, and just a few days ago, we placed it on our first Christmas tree.

Matt touched my shoulder. "I'll leave you alone while I make sure the grounds are secure."

I nodded and continued to read:

In your letter, you called me the light of your lives. But I'm not that light. All glory to God. I'm just happy I'm the instrument He used to place the Light into your hearts. Christ is like the beacon in that wonderful lighthouse. Only He can lead you to a life of peace no matter your circumstances.

I continue to pray that God will deliver a precious child into your loving hands. The Great Physician is capable of healing Henny's womb but lean upon God. He often has better plans for us than we could ever know.

Merry Christmas.

Beatrice

December 22, 1956

Matt's footstep echoed on the wooden porch. When the door opened, free-flowing tears prevented me from turning to him.

He touched my shoulder as he came behind me. "Pops told everyone his testimony," he said. "about how this sweet lady and her husband honeymooned nearby. Pops had just learned of his transfer from duty here, had no idea where the Coast Guard would send him, and Grandma had learned she could never conceive. The woman prayed with them and listened. She told them about the Light of the world, and they did the listening. For Christmas that year, they received genuine peace."

"Did you know she was my grandmother?" I handed him the letter.

He tucked it into the case, locked it safely inside, then turned to face me. "Yes, but not because of the letter. Grace . . . Lauren and I are friends."

My mouth hung open.

He winked. "Your grandmother's prayers are the reasons I'm here."

I cleared my throat. "The reason you were born?"

"No, that would be God." He scrunched his face and pretended to knock on my head as if listening for a hollow sound. "The reason the Light led me here—to my roots. Let the tour guide tell you the story of a five-year-old boy called James who used to hang out here and visit Lester Sanderson. He'd bug the man to death. Lester spent hours with him though he was supposed to be working. One day, the woman Lester thought was the boy's mother came to take him home. She told Lester that James was an orphan in her temporary care. Lester and Henny ended up adopting him. James is my father. Then years later, Lester and Henny got a letter from your grandmother to say that she had heard from Lauren about the trouble their grandson Matt was in, and that she was praying for him."

"H—how do you know Lauren?" I asked as we walked back along the pathway and into the gift shop.

"We both landed in the same place around the same time—a safe haven in Colorado—with a mutual friend of our grandparents. Flo taught us both to trust in God again. Lauren was dealing with—well you know. But she hadn't invited the demons into her life with bad choices—the way I'd done."

Lauren hadn't invited them in. I was just beginning to understand that I had invited the evil into her life. "Are you—do you see Lauren?"

"I haven't seen her since I left Flo's. We keep in contact though." He looked away and then back to me. "She is beautiful—like her twin. Lauren always said you and I'd like each other if we met."

Lauren had been right. I liked Matt—very much. But why couldn't my sister have loved someone as gentle and sweet as this man?

Because a guy I'd considered my boyfriend had violated her in the worst way.

I shivered at the thought and looked around the empty gift shop. "I'd hoped to say good-bye to your co-worker."

Those eyebrows came together again. "Co-worker?"

"Yes, an elderly man. A woman, too."

"George? I didn't see him, and the woman was probably our crazy pelican lady."

"They were in the clearing when we were in the tower."

"Oh, that's who you waved to." He stepped beside me. "Don't be a stranger, Grace. If you come back, I'll take you to dinner."

"It's a date." Warmth surged into my cheeks. I'd never been so forward.

"It is a date," Matt said. "Let me walk you out."

I stopped when we reached the Christmas tree. I touched the aged hand-painted lighthouse ornament and was surprised when Matt's fingers brushed against mine. "Pops painted these—a lifelong hobby. He sent one similar to this to your grandmother."

I took a deep breath. "And you donated these, right?"

He tilted his head, and again the lopsided grin brightened my mood. "How'd you know?"

I stood in silence for a moment before saying good-bye and going to my car. On my seat, a brightly covered package gleamed in the glow of the streetlamp overhead. "Matt," I whispered. He had to have placed the small wrapped box in my car before he'd greeted me in the gift shop.

I ripped open the gift to find a lighthouse ornament similar to the one in the gift shop. A card lay underneath. "Peace I leave with you; My peace I give you: I do not give to you as the world gives. Do not let your hearts be troubled, and do not be afraid. John 14:27" Love, Lester and Henrietta Sanderson (Mrs. S.) and Matt.

Peace. It was as elusive as the Light. I was starting to see that I needed both, but how was I to find them? Find Him? I backed my car and pulled closer to where Matt waved good-bye from the gift shop porch.

"Dinner. Movie. Date," he called.

I leaned over to look at him. "You bet, and please, tell your grandparents I said thank you for the beautiful gift."

He scratched his head, eyebrows tilted downward.

"Merry Christmas." I pulled away with a smile. He'd almost had me believing George had been his helper and the elderly woman had been the hunter of an ethereal pelican.

"Of Christmases past, maybe," Matt had said of his belief in ghosts.

I braked before turning onto the road and thought about going back to ask him.

Instead, I opened up my purse and pulled out the next envelope. Matt was a mystery I looked forward to solving.

But first, on with the treasure hunt. "Where to next, Grammie?" I looked to the heavens and pulled out onto the street.

Chapter Eight

Debbie Roome

New Zealand

The flutter of little feet drew me out of deep sleep.

"She's awake!" A child's high-pitched voice pierced through the last remnants of drowsiness. The feet and voice receded. "Granny, come! Aunty Grace is awake."

Light streamed through an unfamiliar window. My head pounded; my eyes ached. It didn't feel as if it should be morning already. Where on earth . . .?

Of course–New Zealand! Slowly the events of the preceding day seeped back into my consciousness: the warm weather, that didn't feel at all like Christmas, despite the baubles and tinsel decorating the airport; the strange local accents; and—worst of all—driving on the wrong side of the road to reach Ngaire's house. As stressful as the drive had been, I had still managed to take in a little of the breath-taking scenery. The ocean had spread like a sequinned mat to the left, sparkling in the brilliant sun, while green hills had unfurled to the right. Farms had dotted the landscape and sheep grazed in clumps.

Ngaire stood at the door now, a large smile on her deep olive face. Her nut-brown hair, streaked with gray, hung in a braid.

"Did this little rascal wake you?"

At Ngaire's side, the little rascal's face was lit up with pride at her accomplishment.

"Well . . . yes. But it's a good thing. The sooner I start operating on New Zealand time, the better."

"I'll brew some fresh tea for you in the kitchen. Chamomile, right? I bought some especially."

I smiled. After a few weeks of being on Grammie's adventure, it didn't surprise me anymore that she had seen to all these little details.

Fumbling for my watch on the bedside table, my fingers instead wrapped around the tiny wooden whale that had been in envelope seven. I traced its smooth shape before putting it down next to the photo of the tree with the spiky red blossoms, the other mystery item in the envelope.

"All to be explained, right, Grammie?" I said aloud to an empty room. Ngaire and her great-granddaughter had already left.

I made my way—somewhat groggily—to the sagging bay window and pressed my face up to the glass to stare out at the ocean. Blue, navy, and turquoise layered the water, and waves washed against rocky cliffs and a fringe of dark sand. How many times had Grammie looked at this same view? Ngaire had told me the night before that Grammie had slept in this room many times in the year she spent as a missionary in New Plymouth. The thought filled me with a strangely conflicting mix of joy and sorrow.

As I dressed, I thought of the warm welcome I had experienced from the moment I had arrived at this home. My first feeling as I drove up the long sandy driveway had been one of trepidation. The weatherboard home, spreading in all directions, looked rather haphazard. Additions had been made over the years and nothing quite matched. I couldn't help but wonder who could live here.

However, Ngaire's warm welcome at the door had eased my apprehension. She had folded me into her arms like a long-lost daughter and had drawn me into her worn, but spotless home where the aroma of home baking wafted from the kitchen. I had been introduced to her large extended family. Her son and daughter-in-law, with their five teenage children, all lived in the house. One of her granddaughter's had 'got herself into a spot of trouble' as Ngaire put it, with the result that a lively two-year-old now also shared the home. "It's crowded but whānau – extended family – is important to us Maori," Ngaire had told me with a smile.

The evening had passed quickly, a blur of smiling brown faces and hospitality. I loved the way they spoke, the lilting accent that ended every sentence on an upbeat. I suspected it was on purpose that Ngaire delegated me as babysitter for her granddaughter's little girl, Aroha. "We'll cook while you watch the little one," she said, depositing the child in my arms. "She's tired so just cradle her, and she'll probably go to sleep."

I admit I hadn't been all too happy to begin with. I knew nothing about babies and small children, and they scared me somewhat. I had leaned back in the armchair, shifting position until Aroha seemed comfortable.

"I like you," she had said, reaching up and

touching my auburn curls. "Your hair is pretty." She entwined her fingers in a spiral and held it firmly until her eyes drooped and breathing slowed. Then her grip loosened, and her hand fell onto my chest, splayed like a tiny starfish.

As I brushed the hair that little hand had clasped the night before, a new—unwanted—thought drifted through my mind. Lauren's little one would be just a little older than Aroha. What kind of conversations would she and Lauren be having? Did she look like us or more like Steve? The sudden yearning to see my sister's child was intense, but I pushed it away as I made my way to the kitchen for my cup of chamomile tea.

"You ready to go, girl?" Ngaire asked when the tea was finished.

"Sure."

"Take a jersey with you. The early morning breezes are fresh on the beach."

We slipped out of the house, and Ngaire led the way to a sandy path. "I often go down to the beach in the morning to pray," she told me.

"Tell me how you and Grammie ended up in mission work," I asked as I strolled next to her.

"It was at a mission house in New Plymouth," she replied. "Bea and I were put together to do door-to-door evangelistic work. She was quite homesick at first, so I brought her home with me on weekends. My mother treated her like a daughter, and we became best friends." Her voice broke slightly, and she gazed upward. "It may sound silly, but I miss her terribly. We hadn't seen each other in decades, but we wrote each other every month. And when e-mail came out, we kept in touch even more often." She stopped walking and looked me in the eye. "She was an amazing woman, Grace . . . and I can see the same strength of character in you."

"Really?" I was still trying to make sense of her words when we reached the edge of a low cliff.

"Be careful down here," she instructed. "The sand is loose, and it's easy to slip."

I was more interested in the trees with gnarled

limbs and weathered trunks that clung to the rocks. Each was crowned with a mass of red blossoms that looked like the ones in my photo. "What are those?" I asked as we clambered down the path.

"*Pohutakawa* trees," she answered. "They're also known as the New Zealand Christmas tree as they flower in December.

"They're beautiful," I said, gazing up through the canopy of red.

"We'll stop here for a moment," Ngiare said. "This is one of my favourite prayer spots." She patted a smooth, gray rock and indicated I should sit next to her. The beach was about a dozen feet below us, and the sand lay flat, its wrinkles and flaws smoothed by the outgoing tide.

"I can see why," I said, taking in the floral beauty, the sparkling waters below. "It's so peaceful here."

"It is today, but it's not always like that," Ngaire said, her expression contemplative. "We have violent storms from time to time and the wind can be very damaging." She seemed to withdraw into her thoughts for a while, and I sat and waited. The sun cast a peachy glow across the ocean, and I felt more at peace than I had for a long while.

"Did Bea ever tell you about the whales?" she asked after a while, angling her head toward me.

A surge of excitement made me sit upright. "No, but she placed a carved whale in the envelope with my tickets to New Zealand."

"She was staying with me one weekend when a pod beached themselves over there."

I followed the direction of her outstretched hand to an expanse of sand. "What happened?" I asked.

"We tried to rescue them. Called in an emergency, and the local radio put out an appeal for people to come and help."

"And?"

"Come." Ngaire stood and started the descent to the beach. "They were pilot whales, a pod of about thirty, and they were stranded just here."

I stood still, wind whipping my hair, salty spray coating my face as I tried to imagine the scene.

"We had a hundred volunteers come out," Ngaire continued the story. "We stayed down here all night, draping the whales with wet towels, pouring sea water over them and turning them so they could breathe more easily." Her eyes misted over, and I felt my own eyes moisten.

"Did you save them?"

"Some. When the tide came in, we managed to refloat those closest to the water but some of them came back. The thing is that they're social creatures. If one of them becomes stranded due to illness or injury, the others will follow. They stick together, so to speak. They won't leave a wounded family member. One of the whales was obviously sick."

I closed my eyes, and for a moment, I had a vision of a beach full of whales, gray skin glistening as people worked to save them. If an animal cares for its own, who am I not to? The thought skittered through my mind, and I pushed it away. *People are different*, I told myself.

Ngaire reached out and took my hand. "Don't fight God, child. If He's talking then let Him talk. And when He's done talking, act on what He's told you."

"I need a few moments," I said, loosening my hand from hers and walking toward the water. I knew that coming to New Zealand would be challenging, but Grammie had got right under my skin this time. As an animal lover, I knew if whales were stranded on the beach, I'd be down here helping them . . . and yet I had no time for my own sister who was obviously hurting. She had to be. "My heart has become very hard," I whispered to God although, since it was the first time I'd talked to Him in years, I wasn't sure He'd be listening. "If you want me to change, You'll have to soften it for me." I stayed on the water's edge allowing the waves to lap at my feet as the sea changed from apricot to gold to silver.

Eventually, Ngaire came to join me, her hand soft on my arm. "Come up to the Pohutakawas, Grace. There's something there for you."

I followed her and after examining the trees in the area th'dat she pointed out, I found a carved Christmas bauble hanging from a low branch. The wood was inlaid with swirls of turquoise and pink shell and had a seam through the center. "Does it open?" I asked.

"Try and see," Ngaire said with a smile.

I twisted the bauble carefully and split it into two halves. A carved wooden whale nestled inside in tissue paper. It was twin to the one in the envelope Grammie had left me. Twin whales. Sisters that would stay with each other to the point of death.

Before dinner that night, I volunteered to babysit Aroha. We sat on the carpet and stacked blocks into towers and then knocked them down before starting over again. She squealed with laughter and tossed her head. "Again, Grace," she shouted. "Let's do it again." We had a great time, but she fussed as her mother supervised dinner and then Aroha's teeth brushing. It was an immense responsibility raising a child, and Lauren was doing this alone . . .

"I never thought of Lauren's baby as being a child, a little person that can talk and laugh and have fun," I confided in Ngaire when the family had gone to bed. I'm still angry with her, but something has started to shift inside me." I hung my head, regret rising like a fountain. "I wish I had a photo of her.

Ngaire smiled. "I can show you a recent picture if you'd like. We can even print it out.

Five minutes later, I sat in front of the family computer while she scrolled through her e-mails. "Here it is," she announced triumphantly after a quick search. "Bea sent this through shortly before she died." The child's face filled the screen; thick dark curls, olive skin like mine, and eyes that danced with life. I had seen that face before. The escape artist, Clara Grace, at the Nutcracker Ballet. I couldn't stop tears from overflowing as Ngaire pulled me into her arms.

Chapter Nine

Joan Campbell

Kenya

"Jambo!"

I hesitantly shook the hand stretched out to me. If his sign hadn't had my name scrawled on it, I would have thought I had the wrong person. Could this middle-aged man be the Constance whom Grammie had told me to e-mail, the one who would meet me at the airport?

"*Jambo*, Grace," he said again.

"Yes. Jumbo. Big plane." I pointed back toward the airport tarmac, wondering how I would survive five days in a country where citizens didn't speak my language. His dark ebony face creased with laughter.

"No, you misunderstand. Jambo is the Swahili greeting." His English was lilting and lovely. "Here, let me take your luggage." I could feel the heat rise to my face and was grateful that his full attention was on my bags.

"Welcome to Kenya," he said when the bag transfer was complete. "I am Constance."

I didn't have the heart to tell him that I had been expecting a woman.

The small travel guidebook I had bought in Auckland informed me that Nairobi was the busiest town in East Africa, and as I stepped from the airport building, I could well believe it. People and their goods spilled from cars, buses, and small vans. Horns hooted, voices called. It was warm, although not as sweltering as I had expected, and the air was laced with the smell of moisture and something heavier and more exotic—flowers, or maybe spices.

"This way, Grace."

Constance led me to an old blue bus, and I nervously watched as two men lifted my bags onto the roof, tying them down with a length of rope.

"What time does the bus leave?" I asked.

"Soon." The driver nodded emphatically. "Less than half an hour."

An hour later we still hadn't moved. My head ached. I was exhausted even though it was early morning. What time was it in the States? My tired brain refused to do the calculation.

"He's waiting for a few more passengers," Constance explained.

Almost two hours later, the bus engine finally—and reluctantly—chugged to life. I was squeezed in between Constance and a large African lady wearing a bright orange head-piece. We crawled through the Nairobi traffic, and I had time to take in the tall buildings, green trees, small shops, parks, and fountains. It was prettier than I had imagined. As we left the city, the scenes became more rural, the poverty more evident. I dozed off, but every now and then I would awake to see rolling green plantations or small towns of brightly colored shacks and open-air markets. We stopped at one of these, and Constance bought some pineapples. They were sweeter and juicier than anything I had ever tasted before.

"Kenya's soil is very fertile. Coffee. Cocoa. Pineapples. The best in the world!" Constance smiled proudly.

By late afternoon, we finally reached Constance's village. My body ached from the long, bumpy drive.

A chorus of young voices welcomed me as I stepped from the bus. "Jambo. Jambo!" and even a few voices saying "Grace!" At an instruction from Constance, the children scuttled backward to give me some space, but their smiles lost none of their fervor. I was reminded of the children in Honduras who had met me with just as much enthusiasm.

One child pointed at me and said something to Constance, who laughed as he answered her.

"What did she say?"

"She wants to know why your hair is different to ours, while Mama Bea's was the same."

"Did they all know my grandmother then?"

"She came often, Grace. Even when she was ill. You don't remember?"

I did suddenly remember. It was after Lauren had left and just before Grammie's diagnosis. She had asked me to come along. "I think you'll be touched, Gracie. They have something we westerners have lost." But I had refused. She had gone alone.

"Your grandparents financed the home these children stay in. In fact, they came one dry season and helped to build it. More than ten years ago. But they also sent cards and letters to the children. They were the children's American grandparents. And whenever Mama Bea came, there was a big celebration. She would bring presents and sweets.

It felt like Christmas to the children."

I became aware that I'd arrived empty-handed.

"I don't have anything for them."

Constance smiled and put a fatherly arm around my shoulder. "No. This time we have something for you."

The crowd steered me to the biggest building in the village—the church—where more smiling faces waited. As I entered the hall, women's voices undulated in the joyful African sound of celebration and several men and women dressed in animal skins performed a traditional dance to the sound of drums and voices. I was ushered to a seat right in front of the small stage and plied with plates of sweets and doughy eats as Constance started to speak.

"It is an honor to have Mama Bea and Baba Joe's granddaughter here today," he said, smiling down at me. "So much of what is good in our village is because of their love. The children's home and school. Even this church, which they helped build with their own hands. And I, Constance, serve the village as a doctor, because they helped pay for my medical training."

Why hadn't Grammie told me all this? Or maybe she had, and I hadn't listened. I remember once flicking through her Kenyan photos as she rattled off a list of difficult sounding names. "It really doesn't mean that much to me, Grammie," I'd said. Shame washed over me as I recalled my indifference.

"Grace. Your grandparents are alive in our village. They live through every orphan given hope and every person saved by my hands. And it is an honor to welcome you here today."

That evening, I was the unworthy guest of honor of the village. Surrounded by their love, I felt like an imposter. I had done nothing to deserve their words of kindness, their songs and poems, their joyful dances. It was Grammie—all Grammie and Gramps—who had left a legacy in this far-flung African village. I had played no part in it, deserved none of their thanks.

That night I slept in Constance's humble home. His daughter slept on the floor so that I could have a bed. It took a long time to fall asleep. One thought kept running through my mind. All those years that I had been steeped in anger and selfishness, living for my own pleasure, Grammie had pushed aside her grief and looked to the needs of others. This village was proof of it. This village was her legacy.

"Grace!" The whisper startled me awake. It took a while to remember where I was.

"Sorry," Constance stood with a torch at the foot of my bed. "But your grandmother asked me to take you somewhere. And she said it had to be at sunrise."

"Sunrise?" My voice was groggy. "But it's still dark."

"It's quite a long walk."

When I emerged from the bedroom, he handed me a steaming cup of coffee. "Kenyan, of course," he smiled.

"The best," we said in unison and laughed.

He led me on a narrow path away from the village. The horizon was lit with a small halo of light. For a while we walked in silence, listening to the African dawn awaken. He knew the calls of all the birds, even imitating that of the tinker, which flew within a few feet of us to fight the imposter male in his territory. The path wound through indigenous forest that Constance and some of the villagers had started to plant twelve years ago. He spoke of his dream to plant more indigenous trees since so much of the forests had been felled to make room for plantations. He let me taste the leaf of a tree which he said was a natural antibiotic and laughed at my expression as the leaf's heat hit the back of my throat.

We seemed to be on a steady downward path, and when we finally broke free of the forest, I saw that a large plain stretched out before us. Between the smaller trees and bushes on the plain, stood a hulking giant.

"What is that?"

"The Baobab tree."

"Wow!"

As we drew nearer to the tree, I gained a better sense of its extraordinary size. Not only was it the height of a four or five story building, it would take about fifteen people joining hands to measure its girth. Its stark branches stretched upward, like hands in supplication.

"This is a young one," Constance said. "They say it is only a thousand years old. There are even larger ones in other parts. Some, three thousand years old."

"Wow."

"This is what your grandmother wanted me to show you. She said you would have seen many trees already on this trip?"

"Nothing like this, Constance."

"The tree is important for us Africans. Many believe that it is the birthplace of humans. One legend tells how God was angry with the baobab because it was always lauding itself over the other trees," Constance continued, "and so God punished the tree."

"How?"

"He pulled it out of the ground and then planted it upside down. Now we see its roots standing in the air."

I thought about being uprooted like that and being thrust into the dark soil, never to see the light again. I knew exactly how black and suffocating it would feel.

"Do you think God does that to people, too?" The words crept out of my mouth before I could stop them, and Constance looked at me for a long time before he answered.

"Not my God," he said. "My God always loves me, even when I don't deserve it. Especially when I don't deserve it." He thought a little longer and a smile crept to his lips. "It's called grace."

Constance said that there were some newly planted seedlings he needed to check on. He left me sitting under the tree, just as the red orb of the sun slipped free of the horizon.

I sat under Africa's beautiful old giant, aware of my own smallness. I thought back on this journey, of all the trees Grammie had led me to: the pine trees of Colorado; the maple tree in which Lauren and I had built a fort; the tree on the ledge at the waterfall, made strong by the beating water; the Nutcracker Christmas tree which had always given us twins such delight; the evergreen at the lighthouse, where I had met Matt, and the blood red Phutakawa trees in New Zealand.

I'm with you every step of the way, Grammie had said. But here—under the ancient tree—I felt another Presence brooding. Maybe I had felt Him all along.

You've taken so much from me. Mom, Dad, Gramps, Grammie. Why should I trust You God?

Why? A flock of birds in the baobab took flight as I flung the words into the sky. *And do You really love me, like Constance says?*

A warm breeze caressed my face. Some clouds high in the sky were tinged with orange and red. For me. God was painting this scene just for me.

I don't deserve Your love, You know. I've ignored You, been angry with You, even cursed You. Why would You still love me?

Grace. Undeserved grace. It was here in the beauty of the African sunrise, and in the voices and smiles of the people who welcomed me yesterday. Grammie's well-planned adventure was filled with her love for me. And now I felt God's love stirring deep in my heart, fanning the almost dead embers to flame.

I'm sorry, Lord. The words flowed out of me, now that the plug of anger was gone. *I needed You so much, but I ran away from the only arms that could have really comforted me. I want to come back to You now. Help me do that.*

As my tears fell on the hard African soil, I felt the solid knot of despair loosen inside me. Light and warmth flooded into me, displacing the suffocating blackness that had kept me prisoner for so long.

Constance found me there as I wept on the ground.

"Gracie!" His face was etched with concern. "What is it?"

"It's good, Constance. I've just been touched by God's grace."

I spent another three days in the warm embrace of the Kenyan village, and when it was time to go, I wept again.

Constance handed me a gift wrapped in large leaves. "One of the children made one of these for Bea the last time she was here. When she told me you were coming, she asked if he would make one for you, too. An African ornament. It will help you remember us."

"How could I ever forget you all, Constance?"

I said, unwrapping the gift.

The ornament was a tree wound from steel wire. A baobab tree. The children had all pressed in around me to see my reaction. One boy, Joseph, seemed to be glowing with particular pride.

"Did you make it, Joseph?" I asked.

The boy nodded, his smile broadening even more.

"I love it," I said enfolding him in a hug. "Thank you."

My luggage was once again back on the blue bus's roof. Every villager had come to shake my hand or embrace me. It took more than half an hour to say good-bye Kenyan style. The passengers on the bus sat watching patiently. I laughed as I thought what would have happened if you held up a bus that long at home. Grammie had been right. These villagers did have something we had lost in our fast-paced, self-centered lives.

"Come back, Grace. Promise you'll come back. The children love you as much as they loved

Mama Bea," Constance said as he waved me off, the children running along beside him waving wildly. "I promise, Constance," I shouted from the window.

At Jomo Kenyatta Airport, I fingered the last envelope. A deep part of me knew just what it held—had known from the time I first read Grammie's letter—and a cold fear crept over me. I had done just what Grammie had asked. I had travelled all over the world on her instructions. Surely, I could go home now? There was no reason to open that last envelope, was there?

I looked at the board of departing flights. One would leave for Houston in four hours' time. I needed to get back to my apartment, to my studies, and to Bertie's job. I'd been gone away too long.

And so I pushed the envelope deep into my rucksack and walked over to the counter.

Chapter Ten

Jennifer Fromke

New York City

Daylight worked its way across my room and around two o'clock, the afternoon winter sun reached the perfect slant to cross my eyes. At least that's what time the clock read when I finally pried my eyes open. Fifteen hours since I crashed on the bed. My apartment never felt so welcome as it did last night, though most of the residents had left for Christmas break already.

I blew out an exhausted sigh. Christmas, and the same sick feeling started churning in my gut.

Without Gram. Rebecca, my roommate, had stepped up as soon as she realized I planned to work through Christmas.

"You have to come home with me. I won't let you spend Christmas alone."

The problem was, I couldn't decide which was worse. Being alone or freeloading off a friend. Of course, they meant well, but who wanted an outsider invading their family Christmas? And after graduation, what would Christmas look like next year without roommates and their kind offers? I scrapped the thought before I followed it to a lonely scenario played out in a Chinese restaurant.

I declined her offer when I learned about her boyfriend's plans to join the family as well. Third-wheel situations cut especially deep since I'd lived most of my life as a twosome. But Lauren made a bad choice. Sure, I'd made bad choices before. But had I actually done anything to break my sister's heart? I wouldn't be so cruel. Not on purpose, anyway.

My gaze scoured the dorm room, tidy desks for once, dirty clothes from Africa, and my empty rucksack. Empty except for the final envelope in the bottom. Dread tore like a jagged knife through my chest. Meeting God in Africa, really hearing His voice in my heart, felt amazing. Wasn't that enough?

I rolled out of bed and dragged myself to the bathroom for a splash of cold water on my face. Looking into my weary eyes, I saw something there I never recognized before. Unwillingness. In Kenya, God showed me grace. But He also made me Grace, a long time ago. Receiving grace is more fun than giving it. And some days, receiving grace is much easier than being Grace.

"Fine!" I shouted at the mirror. At God. Almost at Lauren. "I'll go. Wherever it is. It's not like I have anywhere else to go anyway."

As I pulled out the envelope, I shook my head, steeling myself against what it held. I knew it would send me to Lauren. I didn't want it to be a white picket-fenced Cape Cod, like we'd always planned. What if she was happy without me?

Like a punch to my gut, the thought stole my breath. I tore open the envelope.

New York City. Why there?

In the taxicab, I gripped the door handle as we swerved through mid-town traffic. Apparently, every person in the city saved their shopping for the last minute. Sidewalks teemed with crowds, steam billowed out of corner food carts and random grates in the street.

A final swerve of the car, and I landed at the curb, staring up at a glassy overhang with a red carpet under my feet. In a daze, I paid the cabbie and wheeled my suitcase through a revolving door which opened into a rounded room, an intricate marble design set into the floor. I raised my eyes to feast on inlaid wooden desks, all rounded like the walls, with cheerful faces standing at my service to check me into the fine, New York Palace Hotel.

"Whoa, Grammie!"

A tall bellman arrived at my side. "May I take your bag, miss?"

A brunette woman with deep red lipstick beckoned me to her desk. "Checking in?"

I shrunk before the opulence of the room. Christmas garland dripped with shiny golden ornaments over every doorway, and a Christmas tree in the center of the room snagged my heart. I hadn't decorated a tree since . . . Pushing the thought away, I smiled at the woman who awaited my response. Yes. The name is Grace Moore. I turned a full circle to take in the room again. How had Grammie done this?

After the doorman exited the room, I spun around toward the bed. A sprig of evergreen lay there, a red ribbon tied at its base. Beneath it, a note.

Gracie,

The Christmas window displays on Fifth Avenue are stunning every year, but I heard the Lord and Taylor windows would be especially wonderful this year. I hope you'll find time to view them.
Love,
Grammie

Barely twenty-four hours after my return from Kenya, all the travel weighed heavy on my shoulders. One look at the giant poofy bed, and I nearly collapsed upon it. But after sleeping thirteen hours last night, who knew how long it would be 'til I woke up this time?

Armed with a map, I marched down the hall, determined to see this through for Grammie. I headed through the lobby toward the Madison Avenue exit but stopped short when I reached the top of the wide, open staircase. A million twinkle lights lit a courtyard just beyond three sets of glass doors. In the center of the square space towered a Christmas tree lit like a giant star. Blazing white lights reflected off shiny red and golden ornaments, creating the effect of a tree on fire.

I plunged through the door and into a surreal fantasy. The three sides of the brownstone Italian Renaissance architecture, which was lit by more twinkle lights on every arch, doorway, and ledge, dampened a giant portion of humbug I'd been lugging around with me.

I finally tore myself away from the stunning courtyard and melded into the sidewalk traffic, still significant, even at eleven o'clock. The twelve blocks flew past, punctuated by chestnuts roasting, horns honking, Christmas music piped out of every department store on Fifth Avenue, and wispy snowflakes drifting through the air. Idyllic Christmas. Idyllic, except for the fact that I walked alone.

Lord and Taylor stood just beyond the next traffic signal when my heart skipped a beat. Would Lauren be there, waiting for me? No. Who would stand out in the cold all night hoping I'd show up? I hadn't even decided to come until a few hours ago.

Several people gathered around the windows, but the crowded sidewalks from earlier in the day had thinned. The viewing area was roped off with an entrance at one end. I entered and peered into the first window.

A log cabin set in the rear showed an imp dressed in sparkly white, peeping out the window, and hiding behind the curtain before she peeped out again. A cozy fire behind her crackled while snow doused the entire woodsy scene. In the far-right corner, under a tall flocked evergreen, hid another imp, or was she an elf? She seemed to be sheltering beneath the boughs of the tree.

The second window depicted a sunny, snowy day, maybe the day after the previous storm. Everything sparkled. Icicles clung to the trees. One of the imps skated on a circular rink, while the other lifted a snow-shoe-clad foot into the air beside a giant sparkly snowman.

A sledding hill dominated the third window. Children slid down both sides of a steep hill, one imp hid behind a tree on one side of the hill and the other rode a toboggan down the other side, hair flying.

The final window presented a white forest filled with flocked Christmas trees, all dressed in sparkling white décor. Each tree was decorated with a different theme: snowflakes, white birds, snowmen, white stars. The two little imps stood together, each held the hand of a little animal, which hung in the air between them. They rotated slowly, gazing in wonder at the surrounding winter wonderland. I studied every tree, working my way across the window. But when my gaze reached the final tree, a short, natural-looking tree in the far-right corner, I froze.

Very few ornaments hung from the tree. The

natural beauty of the fake-snow-laden deep green boughs almost hid the tiny treasures. How could it be? Treasures I had carefully wrapped in tissue and carried in my handbag through the airport. Every ornament from Grammie's Christmas odyssey hung on this small tree.

I looked over my shoulder, expecting Lauren. Expecting someone. But very few peopled the sidewalk. Even the traffic had grown sparse. What did it mean? I looked back across the four windows. A young couple huddled together, whispering before the first window. Streetlights reflected in the moisture on the street. Footprints marked the snow, just beginning to collect on the sidewalk. No one looked my way.

Transfixed, I stared again at the small tree on the other side of the glass. Probably no one else would even notice it. No doubt it had been placed there for me. But I couldn't reach it. Trapped behind a glass wall.

The circular ornament from Flo's place in

Colorado hung at the top of the little tree. The circle made from three beautiful strands. Grammie, Lauren and I used to be a threesome. The fearsome threesome. Grammie used to quote that verse about a cord of three strands being hard to break. Then she'd always say, "That's why we three have got to stick together. To keep each other from breaking."

I reached my hand toward the tree, pressed my fingertips against the glass. The ache in my heart twisted sharply. So close, but not close enough.

Grammie, I don't get it. Every other place you sent me, there was a person there to explain. Now I'm in the middle of a huge romantic city that glistens at Christmastime and I've never felt more alone in my life.

Christmas Eve dawned with clouds and wind. A view of the street from my window showed snow gusting around corners and people bundled up

Eskimo-style. Breakfast arrived on a tray accompanied by another sprig of evergreen and a note. Chamomile tea and crispy croissants. Thanks, Grammie.

Grace,

> *Enjoy your day shopping and seeing the sights. At dusk, I think you'll find the Lincoln Center tree breathtaking. It's supposed to be blue and silver this year. You are looking for something small and silver.*
>
> *Don't forget to squint. (wink)*

Love you,

Grammie

I wandered through the day, not buying Christmas presents. As darkness fell, a weariness crept into my bones. Another lonely Christmas, and this year I couldn't even pretend to enjoy it since there was no one to pretend for. The doorman hailed a cab, and I sank into the slippery leather seat for the ride across town to Lincoln Center.

Happy people rushed through the streets toward home. Tears pricked my eyes, unbidden. The dark road into my future loomed ahead of me like a curving road at night. Dark trees on either side, but no homes. No lights. I'd always had a place to stay, but since Grammie died, the simple word "home" had lost its meaning.

City lights blasted, multi-colored, flashing. Spotlights lit entire buildings. Snow continued its gradual fall, and streetlights took on a glow reminiscent of old-fashioned paintings. The cab swung into Columbus Circle and the corner of Central Park whooshed by the window. Just enough snow had fallen to cover everything. White outlined black branches, tiny twinkle lights lit trees in varying colors, and snow flocked the evergreens. Unspoiled. Romantic. Like a movie. With me on the outside, looking in.

"Lincoln Center," the cabbie mumbled into his shoulder as he pressed a button on the fare box.

I fumbled through my pocket for some cash and stepped onto the curb. A huge tree rose up in the courtyard between the Philharmonic and the Metropolitan Opera House. I crossed the street, mesmerized by the bright blue lights. Remembering Grammie's note, I squinted. Driving through the dark on snowy nights at Christmastime, Lauren and I always squinted at the Christmas lights we passed along the way. Somehow, it made everything seem more magical. I opened my eyes. No extra magic here.

As I drew near, I could see the ornaments on the tree were mostly shiny and silver and probably twelve to twenty-four inches high. They reflected the blue lights like mirrors, creating a stunning effect that seemed to fill the huge space, bordered on three sides by hulking sixties-style architecture.

The base of the tree was surrounded by a wooden structure, three feet high, painted white. And five feet out from the tree stood a temporary metal fence, like you might see at a construction site. And Grammie wanted me to find an ornament here? Great.

I reached the metal fence and wrapped my hands around the top bar. Icy cold seeped through my gloves and shot up my arms, but I froze in place. The tree stood beyond my reach. If I could even see the ornament Grammie wanted me to find, I'd never be able to grab it.

City noise dampened under the falling snow. A man in a long wool dress coat double-stepped across the square. A security guard meandered along the Philharmonic side. I shrugged and started rounding the tree, scouring its lower branches for anything small and silver. Halfway around the tree, a shimmer caught my eye. Small and sparkling, a snowflake twirled beside a giant glittering star. Out of reach, like the tree in the window. *What's your point, Grammie?*

A twinge of ice chipped off my heart as the snowfall increased, falling from the sky in clumps. I turned my palm up to capture a clump and then held it close to view. Just like the first time Mom showed us how to do this, I scrutinized the individual flakes and tried to separate them on my dark glove. Even the tiniest flakes had their own shape, their own unique design.

"No two snowflakes are the same. See?" Mom had pointed to the snowflakes on her mitten, showing Lauren and me.

I remember not saying anything but looking intently at the snowflakes in my hand. Trying to find two that matched. To prove Mom wrong. But she had been right.

Mom had pulled two small packages from her pocket and handed them to us. We both tore open the small tissue-wrapped gifts. I pulled out a shiny silver snowflake on a chain then checked to look at Lauren's. A habit of mine—checking to make sure we both had the same thing, the same amount, identical shares. While similar to mine, the snowflake on Lauren's necklace was cut into a different shape.

A tornado had spun inside my chest, but before I could voice a complaint, Mom pulled us both into a hug. Her calm voice soothed my frayed edges. "You two may look the same to most people in this world, but each of you was handcrafted by God to be utterly unique. Like snowflakes. And I'm grateful He made you each so special."

"We're like snowflakes?" Lauren had said. Her big green eyes nearly popped out of her head.

I loved Lauren's snowflake. I swallowed my disappointment and studied my own. The outer shape resembled a diamond. Hers seemed more intricate, with six sides and a lacier appearance.

I stared at the beautiful snowflake ornament hanging on the Lincoln Center tree. Only six feet away, but beyond a barrier. Intricate glass, with tiny details. Six sides, and so many facets, it captured blue light from the tree, twinkling as it turned in the icy breeze. My hand clasped the snowflake around my neck.

A cozy flame kindled in my heart. That

snowflake ornament would match Lauren's necklace perfectly. The empty courtyard stretched around me like a vast lonesome prairie. With almost every sound muffled under a blanket of snow, my toes stung from the cold. I checked over my shoulder and stared into the eyes of a tall black man, the security guard I'd seen when I first arrived in the square. My heartbeat slammed my chest wall. Where had he come from? And how was I going to get that ornament now?

"Good evening, ma'am. It's a beautiful tree."

"Yeah." Disappointment oozed out with my voice. I was so close.

"What's a pretty lady like you doing her all alone on Christmas Eve?"

I must look pathetic. I sighed. Might as well tell the truth. Nothing left to lose. "Can you see that little snowflake ornament? The one that looks like it doesn't belong?"

"Sure do."

"Well, I think my Grammie hung it there for

me to take." I gestured to the fencing and then to him. "But it looks fairly well-guarded."

He stood at attention and saluted. "Thank you very much." He relaxed, standing at ease like a military guy, and his face broke into a smile. "Would you mind if I asked your name?"

Why not? "Grace."

He nodded thoughtfully. "Would you happen to be Grace, of the Bea Whitman and her twin granddaughters' fame?"

I looked up as relief poured across my shoulders. Of course, Grammie would make a way for me to receive this ornament. She'd planned everything else out to the smallest detail. How could I doubt her now? My mouth dropped open, but words wouldn't form at first.

He laughed. "Go ahead." He moved the metal fencing so I could slip through. The ornament hung just above my outstretched arm. On tiptoes, I reached and grasped the snowflake.

"Thank you so much! Thank you for this." I

held up the ornament, and as it dangled, blue light from the tree sparkled through the faceted crystalline snowflake.

"You are very welcome. Bea's network of friends alerted me of your progress in the treasure hunt to make sure I'd be here when you arrived. To guard your ornament. To make sure you received her last gift. Merry Christmas."

"Merry Christmas." My voice sounded small in the big empty square. The security guard wandered away toward the opera house behind me. I walked in the opposite direction, gazing at the beautiful ornament in my hand. Powdery snow fluffed around my boots with every step. I glanced over my shoulder again, but only empty footprints followed. My hurried steps carried me away from the beautiful tree, but where would they lead me now?

This trip came from the last envelope. My feet stopped at the thought. Grammie's last note . . . her last gift . . . it was over. This was it. A twinge squeezed my heart. I turned the ornament over in my leather-clad hand. Grammie's adventure sent me all over the world, to meet wonderful people who all pointed me further along the journey.

God's presence in Kenya woke me up from the nightmare I'd chosen to wear like a cape. But at journey's end, I stood alone in a vast city with a new collection of Christmas ornaments . . . and still alone. Grammie had said she'd be with me every step of the way. And I'd felt that. But now that it was over . . . Was it over? A yearning from the center of my being blew against me like an icy gust of wet wind. I needed to find Lauren. Did I even have her cell number?

I whirled around, searching the square. Grammie sent me here. She had to know. I desperately wanted her to know I'd need Lauren tonight. Only a few people walked the sidewalks and every one of them looked to be in a terrible hurry.

Snowflakes globbed onto my eyelashes,

melted on my cheeks, mixed with hot tears. Removing a glove, I traced the stunning glass ornament. A tiny high-pitched voice split the hushed square.

"Mommy, look!"

Across the plaza, a little girl pulled on her mother's hand, dragging her through the snow. She pointed at the tree. "The snowflake is gone! Is she here?"

I took a step closer. Something dangled from the little girl's hand.

The mother scooped the child into her arms and swiveled around.

My gaze locked with that of my twin for the first time in years. Falling snow cushioned our steps as we drew near in silence. What do you say to the person you love best in the world but have only just stopped trying to hate?

The rest of the city fell away. My heart pounded against my chest. I closed the distance between us, crunching across the snow, and bent to look Clara Grace in the eye. "What a cute little monkey! Your mom and I used to have matching ones just like it."

The Greatest Treasure

The authors who collaborated on The Christmas Tree Treasure Hunt hope that you have enjoyed our stories. In Grace's travels, she received the gift of friendship, the gift of knowledge, and the various presents her Grammie left for her along the way. However, the greatest treasure Grace received is a gift that is available to all of us: forgiveness.

You see, the real Christmas story is much more than a tale of a husband and wife traveling to Bethlehem to pay their taxes and so much more than a woman giving birth in a lowly manger. The Christmas story is the truth about God's greatest gift to mankind: His Son.

John 3:16 tells us, "For God so loved the world that he gave his one and only Son, that whoever believes in him shall not perish but have eternal life."

That Babe wrapped in swaddling clothes, lying in the manger was the most precious, most valuable present God could give—Himself—a sacrifice to the world for the sins that beset us, for the wrongs that we cannot right ourselves. Christ came, He died, and He rose again, victorious over sin and death—the perfect sacrifice for you and me. Why? Because we are unable to save ourselves.

A gift is only a gift if it comes without price to the receiver. But, oh, what a price our Lord and Savior paid when He came to this earth to save us all from our sins.

In The Christmas Tree Treasure Hunt, Grace's forgiveness of Lauren comes from a heart born of gratefulness. Sometimes, we forget what our Heavenly Father sacrificed for us so that we might know His forgiveness. We hold tight to the anger and bitterness when we are wronged or when we feel we are wronged. In understanding the deep nature of God's forgiveness, we should also forgive others. In the forgiveness of others, we can truly find peace—just as Grace has done.

Christmas is a season in which we begin to think about new beginnings. How better to begin anew than to begin with forgiveness—that offered to you by God, through the gift of His Son.

As you study on this—the world's greatest gift—it is our prayer that you will bow your head in meaningful prayer and ask God for His forgiveness. Ask Him to fill Your heart with His presence and to reign as Lord in your life.

And if you have done so, we would love to pray for you and rejoice with you. Send us an email

though our editor, MarjiLaine@writeintegrity.com
and share your story with us.

About the Authors

Joan Campbell

Joan Campbell lives in Johannesburg, South Africa, with her husband Roy, and a goofy Golden Retriever called Jabori (the name means Comforter in Swahili)—the surrogate child since their two daughters left home to study.

Joan is passionate about storytelling, and her fictional worlds are rich with quests and heroes, intrigue and adventure. Her fantasy trilogy, The Poison Tree Path Chronicles (Enclave Publishing) tells the story of a young woman's quest for freedom and redemption, even as she is entangled in uncontrollable magic and a battle-scarred world. Chains of Gwyndorr (Book 1) won the 2017 Illumination award for Young Adult fiction.n Heirs of Tirragyl (Book 2) and Guardian of Ajalon (Book 3) completed the trilogy, which one reviewer described as "a phenomenal work of Christian fantasy, interweaving courage, heroism, sacrifice, and loss to finally reveal the King–the deepest source of hope, strength and love."

Joan's book *Encounters: Life Changing Moments with Jesus*, is a collection of short stories, reflections, prayers and art, based on the lives of people who encountered Jesus during his time on earth. Since the stories are told through the eyes of these individuals, readers are transported into the heart of familiar Bible scenes to experience the person's life-changing moment with Jesus in a wonderfully unique way.

The popularity of Encounters encouraged Joan to write a second book based on the lives of Bible characters, this time drawn from both the Old and New Testament. *Journeys: On Ancient Paths of Faith* releases in November 2019.

Joan is a contributing devotional writer for The Upper Room and Scripture Union and a workshop facilitator for MAI, a ministry which trains and mentors Christian publishers and writers internationally. This ministry has taken her to some remarkable places including Kenya (inspiration for her chapter in The Christmas Tree Treasure Hunt), Ghana and Singapore, as well as enriching her life with friendships across the globe. Find her at joancampbell.co.za.

Jennifer Fromke

Raised in the Midwest, Jennifer Fromke quit pre-med and followed her heart when she studied English Literature at Wheaton College in Illinois. She blinked and found herself living in the South with a cedar chest full of wool sweaters and an aversion to sweet tea. She writes from North Carolina, where the skies are blue, flowers bloom all winter, and the summers are so hot she writes in the shade of her back porch, literally sweating over each novel. Learning to cook cheesy grits smoothed the transition, and now she's living the dream with her husband of 27 years in a recently emptied nest.

Jennifer writes women's fiction about strong women making tough choices. She talks about books ad nauseam and recommends them to everyone she meets, earning her the moniker: The Book Matchmaker. You can follow her reviews on her blog: shetalksbooks.com. Her first novel was published by Write Integrity Press, LLC, and her next three are in the prep kitchen, awaiting their turn in the oven. Her Christmas short story, Special Delivery, is available from Amazon.

Jennifer is an active volunteer with the Women's Fiction Writers Association as well as a local anti-trafficking organization, Present Age Ministries.

Sheryl Holmes

Sheryl Holmes, a daughter of the King and a cancer-survivor, enjoys a loving marriage with her husband of twenty-six years. She is a devoted mother of nine and is currently home educating five of her children.

Sheryl serves an active member of Dwight Chapel's Christ Community Church in Belchertown, Massachusetts.

Sheryl says, "I lift my hands in praise to my Abba Father, and I thank Him for what He has done and for what He has not even yet done, but will do, because I trust Him."

Deanna Klingel

Deanna K. Klingel was raised in a small town in Michigan. She left for college, married, and spent the next twenty years moving every two years with her IBM husband Dave. Their family grew with each move. They  eventually settled in Atlanta with their seven children where they put down roots for nineteen years. The children grew up, left home, and Dave retired. They moved to the quiet mountains of Western North Carolina. It was here, in the quiet remote setting that Deanna returned to her love of writing and began the life of a writer.

Her books include *Beth's Backyard Friends* and *Rebecca & Heart*, both eBooks on Storyrealm.com. She also published award-winning short stories that can be read on her website. Other published books are *Just for the Moment: The Remarkable Gift of the Therapy Dog*, *Avery's Battlefield*, *Avery's Crossroad, Bread Upon the Water*, and *Cracks in the Ice*. Deanna writes primarily for young adults in a Christian market.

Visit Deanna's website at BooksByDeanna.com.

Marji Laine

Marji Laine considers herself a graduated home-schooling mom of four amazing adults. She and her husband of thirty-plus years live near Dallas, Texas with their two dogs and one daughter in college that is allowing them to avoid the empty nest syndrome for just a little longer.

The senior editor of Write Integrity Press, LLC, Marji spends her days reading and editing the amazing stories of her authors. She loves her job! However, getting the chance to write her own romantic mysteries and suspense novels is like having a vacation. Penning a story with unexpected twists and hidden whodunnits is sheer bliss for her.

She enjoys acting in stage productions and teaching at writing conferences. In her spare time, she loves game night with her family and friends, she enjoys singing in her church choir, and leading a high school Bible study in her home.

She prefers mountains to beaches, dogs to cats, NASCAR, white roses, Magnolia Pie, Hallmark Movies and Mysteries, Bath and Body Works, and the color green.

You can usually find Marji tapping away at her keyboard in her favorite recliner with her rescue dogs at her feet. You can also find her at MarjiLaine.com where you can sign up for her newsletter and learn about her most recent romantic suspense, *Breaking Point.*

Fay Lamb

Fay Lamb is the only daughter of a rebel genius father and a hard-working, tow-the-line mom. She is not only a fifth-generation Floridian, she has lived her life in Titusville, where her grandmother was born in 1899.

Since an early age, storytelling has been Fay's greatest desire. She seeks to create memorable characters that touch her readers' hearts. She says of her writing, "If I can't laugh or cry at the words written on the pages of my manuscript, the story is not ready for the reader." Fay writes in various genres, including romance, romantic suspense, and contemporary fiction.

Fay Lamb is an author, an editor, and a teacher. She also loves to teach workshops for fiction writers.

Fay has contracted four series with her publisher, Write Integrity Press. Amazing Grace is a four-novel romantic suspense series set in Western North Carolina. Her The Ties that Bind contemporary romance series is set in Fay's own backyard of Central Florida.

This author keeps busy. Her first novel in the Serenity Key series is the epic, *Storms in Serenity*. The other series is Mullet Harbor, a series of Christmas romances set in the Florida Everglades. *Christmas Under Wraps* is now available.

Fay has an adventurous spirit, which has also taken her into the arena of non-fiction with *The Art of Characterization: How to Use the Elements of Storytelling to Connect Readers to an Unforgettable Cast.*

Fay loves to meet readers, and you can find her on her personal Facebook page, her Facebook Author page, and at The Tactical Editor on Facebook. Fay also invites you to visit her website and sign up for her newsletter at FayLamb.com.

J.A. Marx

J.A. Marx is a freelance editor, writing mentor, and multi-published author. She writes from Texas where she enjoys spending time with her children and grandchildren. Over two decades in Christian ministry, church leadership, and mentoring has given her a desire to see people come into freedom in Jesus Christ. As a digital missionary, her motto is *Equipping the saints, one book at a time.*

Connect with J.A. at jamarx.net.

Ruth O'Neil

Ruth O'Neil was born and raised in upstate New York and attended Houghton College. She and her high school sweetheart have been married since 1991 and reside in Virginia. She has been a freelance writer/editor for more than twenty years and has published hundreds of articles in dozens of publications. Besides freelancing, she has written two stand-alone novels in the What a Difference a Year Makes series (*Come Eat at My Table* and

Belonging), numerous devotionals, and a couple of children's picture books. She is the author of the Spiritual Insights from the Classics series, which are devotional companions to classic literature. Books in this series include devotional companions for *Little Women, Wizard of Oz, 20,000 Leagues Under the Sea, Charlotte's Web, A Wrinkle in Time,* and *The Hound of the Baskervilles. The Wind in the Willows* will be released soon.

Ruth also teaches Writer's Forums to help want-to-be authors break into print with either freelancing or book publishing.

She is a veteran home-school mom, teaching her kids at home for twenty years. Several years ago, she began teaching writing classes at a local home-school co-op. Here she now teaches younger writers to develop their own freelancing career, write their own novel, or create their own picture book. Teaching the next generation of writers is probably the most fun she's ever had!

When she's not writing or teaching, Ruth spends her time cooking for others, quilting, reading, scrapbooking, camping, and hiking with her family.

You can find Ruth at ruthoneil.weebly.com.

Debbie Roome

Debbie Roome was born and raised in Zimbabwe and later spent fifteen years in South Africa. In 2006 she moved to New Zealand with her husband and five children. Writing has been her passion since the age of six and she loves to write stories that touch people's lives and turn them towards God.

Over the years she has won many awards and trophies for her work, including placing first in the

Rose & Crown Novel Writing Competition in 2009 and 2012 and second in the Faithwriters' Page Turner Contest in 2010 and 2014. In 2015 she placed first in the Faithwriters' Page Turner Contest.

Her novel Contagious Hope was a finalist for the Australasian CALEB award in 2013. Debbie's writing has opened doors for public speaking, and she is often asked to share her life story and her experiences as a writer.

Visit with Debbie at
https://www.debbieroome.com/

Christmas Books

If the mayor, the county sheriff, and the pretty school teacher can't keep him out of prison, his nephew might face a worse fate.

English professor, Christian Abrams has thrown his career away to protect his young nephew, Dylan, from an unjust system.

An ultimatum, a threat, a deep secret, and an overprotective mother light up more than Christmas trees in this holiday romantic comedy.

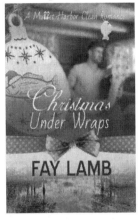

A grieving young woman tells the story of how she met her adopted grandmother. It all begins with an injured veteran, a cranky retired fashion designer, and a lap dog in an elevator at Christmas time.

Making Christmas more meaningful for families.

An advent devotional for families. Each of the twenty-five days of Christmas includes a story, a devotion, an activity, and a song which draw everyone closer to Christ and the true meaning of Christmas.

Lasting friendships can be found in the most unlikely places when you let the Spirit of Christmas guide your heart all year round. This is the lesson brought to life in "Spirit, the Tiny White Reindeer" by Deanna K. Klingel. Beautifully illustrated by Steve Daniels, "Spirit, the

Tiny White Reindeer" is certain to become a Christmas classic treasured by the whole family.

**Thank you
for reading our books!**

**Look for other books
published by**

Write Integrity Press
www.WriteIntegrity.com

Made in the USA
Lexington, KY
14 December 2019

58550923R00107